JENNIFER S. ALDERSON

Death on the Danube

A New Year's Murder in Budapest

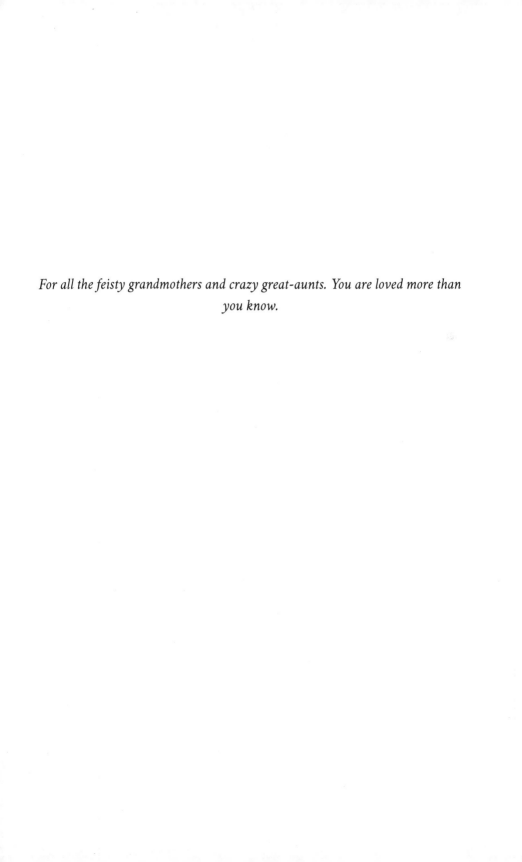

For all the feisty grandmothers and crazy great-aunts. You are loved more than you know.

Contents

1

A Trip to Budapest

"You want me to go where, Dotty? And do what?" Lana Hansen had trouble keeping the incredulity out of her voice. She was thrilled, as always, by her landlord's unwavering support and encouragement. But now Lana was beginning to wonder whether Dotty Thompson was becoming mentally unhinged.

"To escort a tour group in Budapest, Hungary. It'll be easy enough for a woman of your many talents."

Lana snorted with laughter. *Ha! What talents?* she thought. Her resume was indeed long: disgraced investigative journalist, injured magician's assistant, former kayaking guide, and now part-time yoga instructor – emphasis on "part-time."

"You'll get to celebrate New Year's while earning a paycheck and enjoying a free trip abroad, to boot. You've been moaning for months about wanting a fresh start. Well, this is as fresh as it gets!" Dotty exclaimed, causing her Christmas-bell earrings to jangle. She was wrapped up in a rainbow-colored bathrobe, a hairnet covering the curlers she set every morning. They were standing inside her living room, Lana still wearing her woolen navy jacket and rain boots. Behind Dotty's ample frame, Lana could see the many decorations and streamers she'd helped to hang up for the Christmas bash last night. Lana was certain that if Dotty's dogs hadn't woken her up, her landlord would have slept the day away.

"Working as one of your tour guides wasn't exactly what I had in mind, Dotty."

"I wouldn't ask you if I had any other choice." Dotty's tone switched from flippant to pleading. "Yesterday one of the guides and two guests crashed into each other while skibobbing outside of Prague, and all are hospitalized. Thank goodness none are in critical condition. But the rest of the group is leaving for Budapest in the morning, and Carl can't do it on his own. He's just not client-friendly enough to pull it off. And I need those five-star reviews, Lana."

Dotty was not only a property manager, she was also the owner of several successful small businesses. Lana knew Wanderlust Tours was Dotty's favorite and that she would do anything to ensure its continued success. Lana also knew that the tour company was suffering from the increased competition from online booking sites and was having trouble building its audience and generating traffic to its social media accounts. But asking Lana to fill in as a guide seemed desperate, even for Dotty, and even if it was the day after Christmas. Lana shook her head slowly. "I don't know. I'm not qualified to –"

Dotty grabbed one of Lana's hands and squeezed. "Qualified, shmalified. I didn't have any tour guide credentials when I started this company fifteen years ago, and that hasn't made a bit of difference. You enjoy leading those kayaking tours, right? This is the same thing, but for a while longer."

The older lady glanced down at the plastic cards in her other hand, shaking her head. "Besides, you know I love you like a daughter, but I can't accept these gift cards in lieu of rent. If you do this for me, you don't have to pay me back for the past two months' rent. I am offering you the chance of a lifetime. What have you got to lose?"

Lana reddened in shame. Her most recent employer, the owner of a kayak rental and tour company located on Lake Union, was unable to pay her salary for the last two months. As mad as she was, she couldn't fault her boss. He had been struggling to make ends meet for months and warned her he may not have enough to pay his debtors and Lana's salary at the end of the year. She had foolishly agreed to stay on, partly out of loyalty and partly out of laziness. If the kayaking business did go belly up, she'd be forced to find a new job. And even though her resume was long and her experiences extensive, her skill set was quite unique and made finding employment a challenge. Especially during the holidays; Christmas had to be the worst time to lose your job. As if the bills weren't already enough, there was all the extra holiday spending to contend with. The only consolation was that Lana didn't have a large family to shower gifts on, nor did she have to splurge on an extravagant present this year for her now officially ex-husband.

Her only income was from teaching one weekly, hour-long class at her friend Willow's yoga studio. And her salary, as agreed upon before starting, consisted of gift cards to NamasTea, cards Willow received in exchange for teaching the tea shop's owner hatha yoga.

The same gift cards now in Dotty's hand.

Dotty pushed the cards gently back into Lana's hands. "The tour group leaves Prague for Budapest tomorrow morning. It's too late to cancel the last six days of the trip. Carl already asked for time off, and I had to say no because there was no one available to replace him. That's why I sent Sally over to join him. I bet he was missing her, having worked three tours back to back, and it being the holidays and all. This should have been their first Christmas together, but my hands were tied. As much as I love leading tours, I hung up my hat last year for a reason. I'm no spring chicken, and the guests do have you running around most of the day."

Lana nodded in acknowledgement. Though Dotty didn't look a day over fifty, she was pushing seventy, and her health problems were starting to stack up. She had been married five times and widowed four, yet had never been blessed with children of her own. However, she was a wonderful stepmother and kept in touch with all of her husbands' offspring, unfortunately now spread across the country. Which was why Lana felt responsible for keeping an eye on Dotty and helping out where she could.

Dotty changed tactic again. "Wanderlust Tours' reputation is on the line! It's difficult enough getting satisfied guests to leave a review. You know the troublemakers are just looking for a reason to complain. Besides, all you have to do is get them from the hotel to the tour bus, chat with them a while, and make sure no one gets lost."

Dotty's pug, Rodney, rose from his blanket and nuzzled Lana's leg with his flat nose, as if encouraging her to say yes. Lana leaned down to scratch his ear, while taking in his knitted sweater decorated with snowmen. It was perfect for a winter morning's walk, otherwise the poor dear tended to shiver his way through the neighborhood streets on their daily wanderings. *It must be one of her new creations for Doggone Gorgeous,* she thought. Dotty's latest passion project was a new company selling natural-fiber clothing and accessories for dogs of all sizes. Dotty and her best friend, Sally, had started knitting the holiday-themed sweaters in November, and there was already a waiting list. The ladies couldn't knit them fast enough. Chipper, Dotty's Jack Russell terrier, danced around Rodney, showing off his tie-dyed hoodie. He clearly couldn't wait for the humans to finish talking so Lana would take them on their morning walk.

What is holding me back from going to Budapest? Lana wondered. Her divorce had been finalized on December 1. Yesterday – her first Christmas without Ron – had been the most painful day of the year. She dreaded going through the same cheery festivities on New Year's Eve as a newly single woman. Who would she find under the mistletoe? No one, that's who.

Her mom, Gillian, was out gallivanting around with her girlfriends, a group of independent women who preferred each other's company to that of their husbands. Last she'd heard, they were at a spa in Taos, New Mexico, celebrating Christmas. After her dad died in a mountain climbing accident twenty years ago, Lana figured her mother would sell his advertising agency and live off the profits. Instead, Gillian had taken over as president and had grown the company into an important international player in the advertising world. They rarely saw each other, though that had little to do with Gillian's intensely busy schedule.

Willow did invite Lana to join her family for New Year's Eve. Their house was perfectly placed to see the fireworks set off at the Space Needle. She and Ron had spent the past three years ringing in the New Year from Willow's balcony, gazing at the gorgeous firework display timed to bombastic music while guzzling champagne. Lana did love Willow's partner, Jane, to bits, but she wasn't sure being around such a loving couple would do her good this year, or make her miss Ron even more. Her divorce was so recent, Lana still had trouble saying the "d" word aloud. To make matters worse, Willow had already hinted that she'd found the perfect man to couple her with. Precisely what Lana didn't need this holiday.

Dotty would be hosting a party for the neighborhood, as she always did for any major holiday. The older lady's parties always brought in a mix of good friends and neighbors without plans. Lana wouldn't be surprised if this year's guestlist included potential suitors for her, as well.

"Tell you what. If you lead this group, I will throw in three months' rent. Though it still won't get you out of dog walking."

"What about Seymour?" Lana couldn't leave her cat in a kennel, but she wouldn't be able to arrange a babysitter at the last minute, either. Neither she nor Seymour would be able to handle him being locked up in a cage and cared for by strangers for a whole week.

"That old rascal is always welcome to stay with me. Rodney and Chipper love to play with him. And that'll give me a chance to try out a new line of nightwear on him."

Lana laughed, already visualizing how Seymour would look in the latest creation from Purrfect Fit, a new clothing line for cats Dotty was toying around with. She never could get her cat to dress up, but Dotty was a pet whisperer – she could get pretty much any animal into any one of her designs.

"Let me guess – you're going to call them 'The Cat's Pajamas'?"

Dotty's eyes widened. "Ooh, that's good. Do you mind if I use it?"

"Be my guest." Lana chuckled, knowing her Seymour would be in good hands with Dotty. And her "boys" – Rodney and Chipper – loved to play with him, at least as much as her cat allowed. Lana had rescued Seymour from a shelter eleven years ago. It was love at first sight. He was a pure black bundle of affection whose purrs and nuzzles often woke her up in the morning. Her ex-husband hadn't been so keen on him, which should have been a sign to Lana. She'd always wondered whether Ron was just jealous of the attention she gave her cat. When she and Ron had traveled for work, saying goodbye to that fur ball was always the hardest part of leaving. Now that she'd lost her husband and her job, she hadn't anticipated going anywhere for a while.

And yet, she was now being offered the chance to do so – and in style, as well. Wanderlust Tours specialized in high-end travel for professionals long on money and short on time. Most of their clientele worked at Seattle's many computer and high-tech companies, meaning a week or two was the longest they would be able or willing to go on vacation. Dotty had said there were always two company guides escorting the group, but that the tours and day trips were led by knowledgeable locals. All Lana would have to do was smile a lot and ensure that the guests had the trip of a lifetime. Easy as pie.

"Dotty, how can I pass up three months' rent and a trip to Budapest. It's a deal." She stuck out her hand to make it official.

"That's great." Dotty pulled her in for a bear hug. Lana's short bob got tangled up in Dotty's chunky necklace as she relaxed into her older friend's embrace, knowing she had made the right decision. At least, until Dotty added, "There's just one little catch – you used to act, right?"

2

New Adventures

After Lana brought Rodney and Chipper back from their morning walk, she towel-dried the boys until they broke away and shook out the remaining moisture from their coats, spraying her lightly. Lana laughed as the dogs scampered away to the kitchen, knowing Dotty would have left a post-walk treat in both of their bowls. She dried herself off, then poked her head into the living room.

Dotty was snoring softly on the couch, her feet propped up on a magazine rack. The last guests had been shooed out at two in the morning, much later than Dotty was normally awake. Lana could imagine the older lady needed the sleep. Lana started removing the snowflake streamers from across Dotty's fireplace when her landlord's breathing changed and she sat up suddenly.

"You don't have to do that. Cleaning up the Christmas party mess will give me something to do today." Dotty cut off Lana's protest by slapping the couch. "Take a seat, I have your ticket ready. While you were out, I gathered up a bunch of information about Budapest. Nobody's expecting you to be an expert; the local guides are all qualified and speak perfect English. But it would be good if you knew a little bit about the places you'll be visiting, if only to put your mind at ease."

Dotty handed her a printout of her ticket, then a stack of travel guides and informational brochures about all the stops the group would be making around Budapest during the last six days of its sixteen-day tour. Luckily

Lana would have a thirteen-hour flight to read up on the city.

And last, Dotty handed Lana a sealed envelope. "Here's five hundred euros for travel expenses. I know those safety experts say not to, but I think it's better to have too much cash on hand, in case there are any emergencies. I also added in a hundred dollars for any last-minute items you may need to pick up before you leave. The hotels are top class; you don't have to worry about taking along soaps or shampoos. You will need pantyhose for the opera and a good pair of gloves for walking around. The winters are bitterly cold there."

Lana took the money without another word, embarrassed that she needed it, yet grateful that Dotty hadn't made her ask for an advance.

Dotty leaned over and pulled two creations out of her sewing bag, tucked as always in the corner of the couch. "Here, I always have a few extra scarves and hats on hand. The wool is a cotton blend so it shouldn't be too itchy. It's what I use for the animals' sweaters."

Lana rubbed the soft thread between her fingers as she took in the gradient of muted blues and greens. She pulled the hat on and wrapped the shawl around her neck. Dotty was right; they weren't as itchy as pure wool. "They are gorgeous, Dotty. You spoil me."

Dotty admired her handwork, nodding in approval. "They suit you. Now you get on out of here," she said, shooing Lana out of the room.

"Thanks, Dotty. I'll get packed up, then start boning up on Budapest." Lana gave her landlord a peck on the cheek and skipped downstairs.

As soon as she was back in her basement apartment, Lana searched through her overcrowded bookshelf until she found a dusty atlas. Its pages were still worn and earmarked from her adolescent daydreams about traveling the world. Dreams that died once she decided investigative journalism was the path for her. And she'd been right; her two awards for excellence in journalism attested to that. If only she could have talked her anonymous source into going on the record, she would have won that libel lawsuit and still be writing for nationally renowned newspapers, instead of living in a widow's basement and scrounging for any work she could find.

Where the heck was Budapest? Lana wondered as she scanned Europe. All she knew about the eastern European city was that Harry Houdini, her ex-husband's idol, was born there. How jealous he would be of her, Lana thought, briefly contemplating messaging him to gloat. Just thinking about the contortionist who had taken her place and what she and Ron might be doing together, though, pushed the idea out of her head.

She soon found the capital of Hungary. Lana traced the Danube River with her finger through the middle of Budapest, then along the country's border with Slovakia and on to Vienna, Austria. The region seemed to be quite mountainous.

Lana turned to her wardrobe and began piling her warmest sweaters, long skirts, and woolen pants onto her bed. She regarded her dresses, hoping they would be sophisticated enough. Dotty had warned her that their trip included concerts and shows in some of Budapest's most famous symphony and opera houses. Seymour curled up on top of a cashmere sweater, purring contentedly as he marked Lana's clothes with his hair. Lana ran her fingers through his silky fur, scratching under his chin.

"I'm going to miss you, pal." She leaned down to nuzzle his neck while gazing at the stacks of clothes on her bed, when the next crisis became apparent. Her only working suitcase was far too small to hold a week's worth of winter clothes. And she hadn't even thought about footwear yet.

Lana glanced outside and saw the weather was unchanged. It was a dreary gray day, typical of Seattle's soft winters.

"I'll be right back." Lana kissed Seymour's ear. He meowed in acknowledgment. Lana threw on her navy jacket and rushed out into the wind and rain. Luckily her apartment was in the heart of Seattle's Fremont neighborhood. Her street was a mix of old farmhouse-style homes with patchwork gardens – such as the one Dotty bought three decades ago – and newly built condos catering to the growing number of techies moving into the funky neighborhood.

Living in Fremont was a dream come true. This neighborhood was the self-proclaimed "Center of the Universe" and one of the most creative areas in the city. To Lana, the highlight was the Solstice Parade, with its puppets, floats, street performers, and the naked bicyclists who always led it.

She turned left at the Statue of Lenin, his hands recently painted red again, then walked past the Fremont Rocket, towards the main street. As she turned onto Fremont Avenue, she passed signs for the upcoming fireworks show, sending a twinge of regret at missing the fabulous display through her. Quickly, Lana chided herself; the fireworks show happened every year. She had never been abroad, in spite of her childhood dreams, and now she was about to embark on a trip to Budapest – a free one, no less!

Though several shops were closed until the new year, Lana knew the local thrift store reopened this morning to profit from the post-Christmas shoppers looking for a bargain. It was bound to have several suitcases to choose from. Lana pulled her jacket's lapels tight around her neck to keep out the drizzle as she walked past a record store, noodle shop, microbrewery, take-away taco spot, and blown-glass studio, until she reached the best thrift store in Seattle – Second Hand Love.

It was a mishmash of treasures and junk – depending on who you asked – that filled two floors. Lana was certain firefighters would get chills when entering. Nothing was sorted; new additions were simply added to whichever room was the least full at the time. Lana greeted the tattoo-covered owner and breathed in the musty smell of disuse. The shop was nice and warm. Lana unbuttoned her jacket and took in the furniture, books, records, knickknacks, clothes, and accessories stacked up all around her. In the first room, she had no joy. There was no luggage to be found. In the second room, she caught a glimpse of a large case underneath a fake fur jacket and orphaned keyboard. It took her a few minutes of shifting and pulling to get it out.

When she did manage to release the suitcase, her first thought was that it was perfect. It was a large case with two wide straps to hold it closed. The brass-plated corners and clasps were scratched and dull, and the leather was so lined it reminded her of a topographical map. *It has character*, Lana thought. When she opened it up, she was pleased to see it wasn't moldy. With the right kinds of cleaners and a little elbow grease, it would be good as new in no time. Best of all, it was covered in old stickers from places around the world. When she had traveled with her ex-husband, she had collected knickknacks and bumper stickers from the twenty states they visited, but she never had anywhere to put them, because Ron forbade her to decorate their van's bumper with them. Lana ran her hand over the sides, dreaming about the places this suitcase had been. Just thinking about the many exotic destinations pictured on its sides made Lana feel lighter and happier than she had in months. If this suitcase had been all over the world, why couldn't she do the same?

Since discovering six months ago that her husband was in love with his new assistant, she had fallen into a rut and needed a new adventure to pull herself out of it. Dotty wasn't just doing her a favor by allowing Lana to work off her rent; she was giving her a chance to start over. She couldn't let this opportunity slip by her.

When Lana carried the suitcase to the cash register, she found that it was a touch heavier than she'd expected and that she'd had to spend more of Dotty's advance than she'd hoped. None of that mattered; she'd already fallen in love with the vintage case. She practically danced her way to Willows Bend Yoga Studio to show off her newest acquisition to the owner and her best friend, Willow Jeffries.

3

Willows Bend

Willow eyed Lana's latest purchase critically. "Did Second Hand Love let you pay by gift card?"

Lana reddened at the thought. In the Fremont district, bartering was a common way of paying for services and goods, especially between owners of the many small businesses inhabiting the storefronts in this colorful neighborhood. Despite its prevalence, Lana preferred to pay cash whenever possible, figuring that when bartering, one person was always getting the short end of the stick.

"No, Dotty gave me an advance on my salary so I could pick up any essentials before I leave tomorrow."

"Oh, hon, it's gorgeous and so retro. But is it practical? Would a backpack have been a better choice?" Willow opened it up and sniffed heavily. "It stinks, but we can fix that. I have a wonderful perfume at home that's really musky. It should mask that musty odor."

Lana rolled her eyes. *Leave it to my best friend to bring me back down to reality*, she thought. Willow was one of the most practical people she had ever met. Oddly enough, she was also one of the most spiritual and definitely the most flexible. Willow was a petite, slender woman with charcoal skin and a multitude of long braids hanging down to her waist. She was wearing her work clothes – spandex tights and a crop top that Lana wouldn't be able to get around her thigh. At five foot seven, Lana towered over her friend.

They had met a year ago, after Lana damaged her shoulder and was searching for a long-term alternative to physical therapy. Willow's yoga class changed her life for the better, allowing her to finally live pain-free. Since then, Willows Bend Yoga Studio had become something of a second home.

Lana gazed at the bright yellow walls, the mandalas and dreamcatchers hanging randomly around the space, the multitude of ivy vines circling the support beams, the colored Christmas lights strung up across the platform, and the mirrors covering one wall. Here she was comfortable and relaxed.

It wasn't just the welcoming space that kept her coming back. There was something so open and warm about Willow's personality. After a few sessions and teas afterwards, they'd become best friends. It was also thanks to Willow that she had met Dotty and found her current place to live. Some days, Lana felt like Willow was the younger sister she had never had.

"You're right. This suitcase is probably not the most practical choice. But it's got history and has survived many successful trips abroad – or at least more than I have, by the looks of it. Besides, these tours are for rich people. I expect there will be a porter to carry our luggage for us. At least, once we get to the hotel."

Willow cocked her head. "I thought you were the porter."

"No, silly, I'm the escort."

Willow raised an eyebrow.

"Tour escort." Lana laughed and slapped her friend's shoulder. "I accompany the guests on their day trips, assist with serving meals, answer any questions they may have about optional extras, and in general make sure they have a good time. It should be pretty easy."

"You've never been out of the United States before. How on earth are you going to answer their questions about Budapest?"

Lana jutted her chin out defensively. "Dotty gave me guidebooks to read, and I can search online or ask the receptionist…" Lana felt the first tear splash on her cheek as her bravado melted. "Oh Willow, what am I getting myself into? I don't know the first thing about leading a tour group, at least not through a city I've never even been to."

Willow wrapped an arm around her friend's shoulders. "Girl, you're going to be just fine. Don't listen to me blather. Dotty's right. You're a natural guide. Your kayaking clients were always giving you large tips and asking for you by name, right?"

"Yeah, I guess you're right."

"And I'm sure Dotty won't tell the group that it's your first time, so they will assume you know what you're doing."

"Fake it 'til you make it?" Lana grinned at her friend gratefully, feeling instantly better about her upcoming journey. Willow was right. She was a great kayaking guide and did love interacting with the clients, more than she had imagined before starting the job. Besides, this trip was only six days long. Nothing could go wrong in such a short amount of time.

"Exactly." Willow laughed as she gave her friend a hug. "Why don't we have a lemon tea and then I'll help you get ready for your trip? I just picked up some fresh ginger; that'll give it a nice zing."

"That would be great."

4

Traveling Solo

December 27 – Day One of the Wanderlust Tour in Budapest, Hungary

Lana rubbed her eyes, then stretched her arms out above her head, smashing her knuckles into the overhead bins. She'd been so jittery on the airplane ride over that she'd had trouble reading and sleeping. Only after the pilot announced that they were about an hour from Budapest did she fall into a deep sleep. The plane's landing gear bouncing off the tarmac at Ferenc Liszt International Airport woke her up.

She had traveled often, but always with her ex-husband, and she had relied on him to take care of their plane tickets, luggage, and hotel reservations. As nervous as she was about navigating Budapest's airport on her own, she was pleased to discover that it was easy. The airport was large and busy, but not dramatically so. Luggage claim had been a cinch to find, and she breezed through customs, to her delight and surprise. In books and movies, foreign customs officers always seemed so mean.

Her new suitcase was on the heavy side, but back at home, she'd figured she only had to drag it to the waiting shuttle bus, where it would be someone else's responsibility. Now, though, as it smashed into her shins for the umpteenth time, Lana realized she might have to rethink her choice of luggage if Dotty ever asked her to lead a tour again. *As if*, she chuckled to herself, fairly certain Dotty would not need her help again.

As she stepped outside, Lana automatically pulled her jacket collar closer. It was cold in Seattle, but here it was full-on winter. A freezing wind tore through her clothes. Snow covered the tops of most buildings, though the streets and sidewalks were slushy from use. She walked carefully towards the hotel's shuttle bus, watching for patches of ice.

Five other passengers were already inside, chatting together in a language Lana didn't recognize. She nodded and smiled, then focused her attention on the window as their driver pulled into traffic. When they approached the city center, Lana pressed her face up to the cold glass, desperately hoping that her fellow passengers weren't members of her tour. She was supposed to be a world-weary traveler, not an enthusiastic newbie.

Lana had originally envisioned Budapest as a city full of gray, Communist-era buildings. But the photos in Dotty's guidebooks were of beautifully maintained neoclassical, baroque, medieval, Gothic, and rococo buildings. Driving through the heart of the city, Lana was glad to see Dotty's books didn't lie. The imposing statues, tiered fountains, captivating monuments, delicate spires, and majestic buildings decorated with snow and sparkly lights made Lana feel as if they were driving through a postcard. Everything was so much bigger than she had imagined. Several buildings seemed to fill an entire city block, and many monuments stretched high into the sky, often topped by a stately figure, angel, or knight.

As their shuttle bus rounded Széchenyi Square, Lana gasped in awe. A massive bridge built from stone arches and long bars of linked metal led across the Danube River. Two fierce stone lions gazed down onto the traffic, almost daring cars to cross it. *That must be Chain Bridge, the first bridge built connecting Buda to Pest*, Lana thought. She held her breath and gazed down into the Danube as they crossed, humming the waltz of the same name softly to herself. The Pest side had been relatively flat, but the Buda side seemed to be a series of hills and patches of forest.

Built high up on the top of Buda Hill was one of the largest palaces Lana had ever seen. *It must be at least ten city blocks long*, she reckoned. She figured it was Buda Palace, the first stop on their tour tomorrow. Lana couldn't wait to visit it. For now, she was satisfied to simply gaze at the busy traffic, jostling pedestrians, and magnificent architecture.

Their shuttle bus wound its way through the slippery switchbacks up Castle Hill and soon stopped at the entrance to a hotel as regal as Buda Palace, yet much smaller. A glass atrium built over the open courtyard was filled with a glorious Christmas tree, fully adorned with embroidered and glass ornaments. Lana let the porter bring her bag to the front desk, marveling as she followed behind. She was stunned by the refined elegance of the building, holiday decorations, and staff. She'd never been able to afford to stay in a five-star hotel before. When on tour, she and her ex-husband stayed in the cheapest hotels possible. Ron would have slept in the van if she hadn't put her foot down and demanded a room. If this hotel was typical of the rest of the tour, this was going to be a heavenly week.

Lana approached the desk shyly, almost afraid to ask whether there really was a room reserved in her name. "Hi, um, I am Lana Hansen. Do you, um… " Lana felt foolish and didn't dare finish the sentence. This must be a mistake. She picked up her suitcase and took a step backwards, just as the receptionist beamed, "Of course, room 15. Can I see your passport, please?"

"Why?" Lana's brow furrowed, certain this was a mistake.

"We are required by law to make a copy of it for our records. All tourists are required to be registered in this way."

"Oh, sure. No problem." Lana felt like a fool. A world-weary travel guide should know that. She turned away from the receptionist and dug through the money belt attached to her waist until she found her passport. Its blue cover was still crisp and unblemished from actual travel. A month before she found out Ron was cheating on her, she had ordered the passport so she could accompany him on his first international tour. The divorce put the kibosh on that.

The receptionist took it and made a photocopy without so much as a snigger. Lana relaxed, letting her first travel mistake slide.

The woman returned her passport and finished checking her in, then handed Lana a bulky gold key on a keychain as big as her hand. "Please turn your key in at reception before you leave the hotel."

Lana looked at her questioningly. She'd never been asked to turn in her keys at Motel One. "Why would I do that?"

"In case you get robbed, the thieves won't be able to access your room," the receptionist explained patiently.

"Of course," Lana said, wondering how often tourists were victims of pickpockets here. Though with a keychain that size, it wouldn't be hard to steal. "Say, do you know which room Carl Miller is in? We are both guides on the Wanderlust tour."

The woman's eyes lit up, and Lana swore her cheeks reddened. "Yes, Carl is staying in room 14, across the hall from you. He was down here this morning finalizing your dinner reservations, but I haven't seen him since." She turned towards the cubbyholes behind her. "His key isn't here, and he's not left a note for you. Would you like to leave a message for Carl, or try his room first?"

Lana cocked her head, confused by the receptionist's familiarity with her fellow travel guide. "You mean Mr. Miller? I'll try his room."

The receptionist blushed, "Of course, Mr. Miller."

Lana hoped the receptionist was just suffering a crush and that nothing had happened between her and Carl. Lana recalled that he was pretty sexy and quite a flirt, which made him popular with women of all ages. Lana knew Dotty adored him, though in a motherly way. Lana never understood the attraction. To her, he seemed too slippery, boisterous, attention-seeking, and self-important. The fact that she had met Carl soon after her divorce may have blinded her to his positive qualities. But Dotty said he and Sally were pretty serious and she expected they would soon be tying the knot. Lana hoped Dotty was right and that Carl would be pleased to see Sally, not feel as if she was cramping his style.

"Do you know in which rooms the other guests on the Wanderlust Tour are staying?"

"Yes, all of your guests are one floor higher – in suites 21 through 29. You are the last to arrive." The receptionist consulted the cubbyholes again. "It appears all of the guests are in the hotel at the moment, in case you wish to speak with them."

"Suites? Oh, I didn't realize..." Lana grabbed her key off the counter, suddenly desperate to see her room. Was she also staying in a suite? Dotty had emphasized the luxury aspect of the tour, but Lana figured she meant the number of passengers per tour would be smaller and the dinners a touch fancier. Dotty hadn't said anything about suites.

Before Lana could pick up her bag, a bellboy grabbed it and lugged it to the gold-plated elevator doors. She followed along, speechless, totally unaccustomed to being waited on. When he opened her door for her, Lana had to pinch herself from shrieking in delight.

Through the floor-to-ceiling windows, she could see the Danube River snaking through the heart of the busy cosmopolitan. Through open French doors, she spotted a queen-size bed with antique armoires on either side. In the adjoining bathroom was the largest bubble bath Lana had ever seen. It was big enough for two, she mused, automatically wondering what Ron would think of the place. Pretty much every hotel room they stayed in as a couple was as big as this suite's bathroom. As tempting as it was to send a photo of this to Ron, she resisted. Their days of sharing a bubble bath were over.

Right now, it hurt to even think about Ron. Mutual friends had let it slip that he was in Aruba for the holidays with his new lover. Ron had always promised to take her to the Caribbean, but they'd never had the time or money to do so. And now, six months into a post-divorce relationship, he was treating his new girlfriend to the trip he'd promised Lana for years. She squeezed her eyes shut and took in a deep, cleansing breath. *Forgot about Ron*, Lana told herself, *you're in Budapest! Enjoy it!*

The bellboy cleared his throat, interrupting her thoughts. He was standing next to the door, waiting. Lana turned away and pulled her money belt out of her pants again, glad Dotty had given her an ample supply of euros. Unsure as to how much he'd expect, she pulled out a ten-euro note and handed it to him with a small bow.

Based on how brightly his eyes shone, Lana realized she had given him too much. *Chalk it up to experience*. She wondered whether she was supposed to keep receipts for Dotty. Too late – the bellboy was already in the elevator.

Her new suitcase was on the bed. Lana stroked the leather surface and chipped stickers of Tahiti, Paris, South Africa, New Zealand, and Peru, stuck on by a previous owner. She couldn't bring herself to remove them, despite their ragged appearance. Perhaps one day she would fill the sides with pictograms of her own journeys – if she enjoyed this one enough to want to escort a tour group again, that is. Leading a half-day kayaking tour was a whole different kettle of fish than being on-call for seven to fourteen days. At least this time she was just filling in for the last six days. Lana figured the guests knew each other well by now, and Carl must have a good idea of who needed the most hand-holding. She hoped she would have enough patience to deal with every problem amicably. Thoughts of her empty bank account reminded her to be on her best behavior.

Lana looked around the room, then sprung onto the leather couch. She could get used to living like this. As she stroked the soft leather, she tried to temper her excitement. She knew she was only here because Dotty was desperate and she was the only one available. The thought made her giggle. This would probably be the only time she would ever be thankful for being divorced and alone during the holidays. Well, not entirely alone; there was Seymour.

Overcome with emotion, Lana opened her iPad and checked the time in Seattle. It was just after midnight. She'd risk it. Lana clicked on FaceTime and crossed her fingers.

After the second ring, Dotty answered, "Hello, Lana! Are you in Budapest?"

"I am, and thank you! Wow, what a luxurious hotel. Now I'm really looking forward to the rest of the trip."

"I do love to pamper my guests and guides. Do yourself a favor and check out the hotel's spa later. It's not as big as the more famous ones, but is delightful. Especially after such a long flight. Oh, ask if Pallav still gives massages. He's the best."

Before Lana could respond, Seymour sprung onto Dotty's lap and stared into the camera. He was wearing the ugliest sweater Lana had ever seen. A snowman with whiskers and cat ears circled his body in bright shades of green and red.

Lana ticked on the screen. "Seymour, buddy! Oh, I miss you already."

He nuzzled the phone, his purr deafeningly loud. Dotty scratched behind his ears.

"What are you wearing, Seymour? You look handsome."

"Isn't it adorable? It only took two cat treats to get it on him. It's part of a new ugly Christmas sweaters line I'm thinking of introducing next year. I figure adults can wear them, so why not our pets?"

"Seymour, honey, I'll have to dress you up more often – with Dotty's help." Seymour's purrs increased in intensity, and he turned to Dotty, pushing his head into her hand.

"If you like this, wait to see what I knitted for the boys." Dotty patted her knee, and Rodney and Chipper tore over to her. She turned the phone so Lana could better see her dogs' outfits. Rodney sported a sweater featuring a dog Santa, and Chipper's featured two reindeers with droopy dog ears and antlers. "I bet they're going to sell like hotcakes!"

Lana wondered whether anyone ate hotcakes anymore. "They're adorably ugly," she said sincerely.

Dotty shone with pride. "I'm especially proud of the reindeer doggies. What do you think? They did take quite a long time to knit. I miss Sally already. She's so much better at knitting details than I am."

They might not have been Lana's cup of tea, but she could tell Dotty had worked hard on them. "They're great. And I bet they will fly out of the store next Christmas. Another win, Dotty."

Dotty smiled in satisfaction. "So, you didn't call to hear about my knitting projects. What can I do for you, Lana? Are you settling in well?"

"I just arrived. The hotel is gorgeous. I feel like an intruder who's going to be kicked out at any moment."

Dotty snorted. "At the rates I pay, they wouldn't dare. No, the hotel's owner is an old friend. I know they'll treat you right."

"That's good to know. According to the receptionist, all of the guests have arrived, including Sally."

"Ooh, how are the lovebirds? Is Carl pleased to not be alone for the holidays?"

Lana smirked.

"Sorry, dear."

"I honestly don't know. I haven't seen him or the other guests yet. That's why I was calling. Should I go knock on their doors and introduce myself?"

"Goodness, no. Let them be for now and get yourself settled. Officially the Budapest leg of the tour commences with the welcome dinner. You'll have plenty of time to chat with them then."

"Great." Lana said, sighing in relief. Dotty had explained in detail what her role as tour escort entailed during the group's excursions, but Lana hadn't thought to ask about the arrival.

"You go enjoy the afternoon. You're doing me such a big favor just by being there. Without your help, I might have had to cancel the last part of this tour and refund everyone's money. In fact, have a massage on me."

"Thanks again, Dotty." Seymour laid his paw on the screen, partially covering the camera. "I miss you both." The words caught in her throat. The truth was, as glad as she was to be here, she had never felt so alone.

Dotty tried unsuccessfully to cover a yawn with her hand. Seymour laid his head in her lap and purred contentedly. "Well, sweetie, it's after midnight, and my bed is calling. We love and miss you, too. But what an adventure you are about to have! You make the most of it, you hear me? I want you to have the trip of a lifetime. We'll talk tomorrow, okay?"

"Thanks, Dotty. Sleep well."

5

Skinny Dippers and Lovebirds

As tempting as it was to explore the city on her own before the dinner, Dotty's mention of a spa in the hotel solidified Lana's plan for the afternoon. After that long flight, relaxing in a sauna or whirlpool sounded like heaven.

On the back of her bathroom door was a wonderfully soft terry cloth bathrobe. Luckily Dotty had warned her about the tour's visit to Széchenyi Spa, otherwise she wouldn't have thought to bring a swimsuit on a winter trip to eastern Europe. She tied the rope around her waist as tight as she could, then followed the signs to the sauna below. As soon as she entered the space, the humidity hit her in the face. Her skin's pores seemed to open automatically as she breathed in the lavender-scented air.

There was a changing room with lockers on her left. Lana placed her robe and room key into one, before grabbing one of the plush towels from a hamper by the door. Several lockers appeared to be in use, but she didn't hear anyone chatting, only soft classical music coming from a small speaker above the door. The hallway was a rectangle with six closed doors; on each was a sign listing its purpose: Finnish sauna, whirlpool, steam room, foot scrub, cold tub, and swimming pool. Lana considered briefly where to start, before choosing a quick swim to stretch her muscles. Afterwards she could relax in the whirlpool.

When she pushed open the door, a woman screamed and Lana saw a flash of skin as the lean stranger ran to cover herself with a towel. Lana turned away so the woman could pull on a swimming suit, gazing up at the murals of bathing goddesses adorning the vaulted ceiling.

"Geez, you really gave me a fright!" The stranger chuckled nervously.

When Lana looked at the woman again, she was wearing a bikini that left nothing to the imagination. She was younger and prettier than Lana, but her face seemed harder somehow, edgier. Her long black hair and sharp bangs reminded Lana of Bettie Page. She hoped that this young woman was not one of the guests on her tour. "Oh, sorry, I uh…" Lana didn't know what to say to the skinny-dipper.

The girl wrapped a towel around herself and speed-walked towards the exit without saying another word.

"Wait, you don't have to leave on account of me," Lana called out half-heartedly, but it was too late. The stranger was already gone.

Lana briefly wondered whether she'd already gotten off badly with a tour guest, but quickly decided it didn't matter. What did matter was that she now had the pool to herself. Lana dropped her towel onto a chair and dove in, crisscrossing the small pool until she was dizzy and her muscles were aching.

Feeling satisfied with herself for having worked out on her first day of vacation, Lana climbed out of the pool and lay out on a reclining chair until her swimming suit stopped dripping. Lana couldn't remember the last time she had been on a real vacation. All of her trips with Ron had been work-related, and they'd never had time to stop and see the local sights. *What a waste*, she thought, glad that this job gave her the chance to vacation as the rich did. So far, it was pretty fabulous. She stretched her arms above her head, feeling her muscles burning. It was time to check out the other spaces.

Lana pulled open the door marked "whirlpool," her muscles already relaxing in anticipation. The bubbling pool filled the small room, its jets already on high. The walls were adorned with the most colorful tiles Lana had ever seen. Steam rose from the water, as well as giggles.

"Excuse me, this pool is occupied." A man's voice rang through the tiled space.

Lana was so intrigued by the walls, she hadn't noticed the couple in the whirlpool. Based on their embrace, Lana was interrupting more than a dip in the water.

"Oh, of course, I'll just be leaving now..." Lana backed out of the space, embarrassed for interrupting them. Only after she entered the Finnish sauna did she realize that the rooms were meant to accommodate several hotel guests at a time, not just one or two. Though part of her wanted to be snide and spring into the whirlpool anyway, she had no desire to share it with a couple making out a few feet away.

Lana hoped that the guests on her tour weren't the lovey-dovey kind. She couldn't take many public displays of affection without crying, she reckoned.

As the hot air penetrated her skin, Lana thought back on the thin folder of information Dotty had given her about her guests – a list of names and passport numbers, but no photographs. Eight had come over with Carl from Prague and arrived at the hotel a few hours before she did. A group of widowed ladies in their seventies was making its annual pilgrimage to the spas and Christmas markets that Europe was famous for. Dotty said they were regulars of her tours and quite particular about the age of their guides. After a younger guide had them racing around the streets of London, they demanded a leader who was more accommodating to their hip replacements and desire to buy many souvenirs.

Which was what had led to Dotty's strangest request. To Lana's chagrin, if any of the guests asked her age, she had to lie and tell them that she was fifty years old. For a thirty-seven-year-old recent divorceé, this was a painful decision. However, the chance to live rent-free for three months and see some of Europe made her swallow her pride and accept Dotty's proposal with grace. And who knew? If she enjoyed the work, maybe Dotty would pay her to lead another tour. Hopefully next time, she wouldn't have to lie about her age or color her hair gray.

Another couple Dotty had warned her about were the Hendersons. They were the oldest regulars of Wanderlust Tours and good friends of Dotty's fifth husband. They loved to be pampered while seeing the world and refused to let the fact that they were in their nineties stand in their way. Though they insisted on being treated as every other guest, Dotty had already asked Lana to keep an eye on them during the trip.

Another guest was a single woman, only twenty-four years old. Dotty said the young woman was a waitress at a local café and had received this trip as a Christmas present from her mother. *Great mother*, Lana thought, wondering whether her own would ever consider giving the gift of travel. Lana doubted that her mother even knew she had once dreamed of traveling around the world. Not to knock Gillian, but her mother had never bought that line about becoming friends with your children. Gillian was always ready with advice about Lana's posture, diet, career choices, and dates, but she had never gotten to know her daughter as a person.

Their relationship did improve dramatically after Lana won her second award for excellence in journalism. But since Lana got fired ten years ago, they'd rarely spoken. When they did, their conversations left Lana feeling like a loser.

Marrying a magician in the aftermath of her firing probably hadn't helped matters. Not that she'd planned it that way. After the newspaper let her go, Lana had trouble finding work. Months of searching had ended with a gig as a box office ticket attendant at a local theater. During an open-mic nights, she'd met Ron.

Ron made her feel special in a way no other man had before. She had never really been fond of magic, but was amazed every time he pulled a bouquet of flowers out of his sleeve or made her wedding ring hover above her hand. And at that time in her life, she'd needed to feel special. Her career as a journalist, her passion in life, was taken away from her with the single blow of a judge's gavel. Her heart and mind were so damaged, and Ron offered her entrance into a colorful, new world. One she never regretted becoming a part of. They had enjoyed nine wonderful years of marriage, and Lana loved performing in shows across the country as his assistant. If only she hadn't twisted her shoulder while crawling out of that water-filled tank, she might still be happy and married to The Great Ronaldo. But no, her replacement had stolen his heart during their first, month-long tour. Ron was so smitten, he had the gall to send her a text message, instead of waiting to tell her face to face that he was in love with another. Nine years of marriage destroyed in a few hundred characters. Despite the pain she felt every time she read it, Lana couldn't bring herself to delete Ron's declaration of independence.

Lana closed her eyes and sucked up her breath. Ron was ancient history. She rose and splashed two scoops of water onto the rocks, reveling in the hissing sound as the hot steam filled the air. Lana inhaled deeply, feeling the burn as it traveled in and out of her lungs.

Two more guests were last-minute additions, a husband and wife to whom Dotty had given a seventy-five percent discount because they were literally taking the places of the two injured guests. According to Dotty, the husband was an acquaintance of Carl's who seemed extremely keen to spend time with him. When she offered him the tour tickets at a significant discount, he had jumped at the chance. Dotty was thrilled. Not only was she able to cover her costs, but she was also convinced they were a shoo-in for a five-star review. The man and his wife were supposedly on the same plane she was, but there were no couples on the shuttle bus.

Lana smiled when she reached the last name on her mental list, another last-minute addition. Sally Simmons was a good friend of Dotty's and one of the sweetest people Lana had ever met. She was homely and rather forgetful, but a wonderful conversationalist and a darling of a lady, one Lana enjoyed chatting with at Dotty's many holiday bashes. As of late, Sally was becoming a more frequent visitor as she was knitting doggie sweaters to help Dotty keep up with the growing demand.

Apparently Sally's presence on this trip was a surprise present to Carl, her boyfriend of nine months. Sally had been astonished and delighted when Carl, fifteen years her junior, asked her out on a date after they met at one of Dotty's parties. Lana couldn't figure out why Carl had asked her out, until she learned that Sally was one of the richest widows in Seattle.

Dotty had confided to Lana that Sally was notoriously bad with men, usually overwhelming them with so much attention they ran away screaming. After she and Carl started dating, Dotty counseled her friend to be less needy. Dotty knew Carl wasn't the type of man you wanted to smother. Yet Sally had such a difficult time at Christmas without him, Dotty had sent her to Budapest to be with him for rest of the holidays.

Lana had also met Carl at Dotty's parties and was one of the few women on the planet who didn't fall for his charms. She still didn't understand what Sally saw in Carl – well, besides the obvious. Admittedly, the tour guide was tall, sexy, and charming, but he could also be self-absorbed and manipulative. In an unguarded moment, Dotty had told her that she had met Carl when he was down on his luck in a casino. Dotty ended up lending him money so he could leave without having his legs broken. She had offered him a deal similar to Lana's: to work off his debt as a tour guide. Though he took the job begrudgingly, Carl turned out to have a flair for organization and stayed on as an employee after he'd repaid his debt.

Dotty did mention that Carl still had trouble staying out of casinos and gambling halls, which may also have spurred her to send Sally to eastern Europe for the holidays. Alone, he might have faltered and gone gambling. From what Lana had read, casinos were abundant in the cities they were visiting.

Lana hoped Sally would be able to keep him under control so she didn't have to. From what she recalled, Carl was a big man, and not one she wanted to have to try to rein in.

Regardless of his bad habits, Lana was glad Carl was here. There was no way she could lead this group of strangers around a foreign city without some help.

6

Welcome to Budapest

Lana rechecked her makeup and hair for the fifth time, uncertain as to how formal this dinner was going to be. Her ex-husband's idea of fancy was shrimp and steak on the same plate. She hoped her dress was appropriate for the evening. She didn't have much in her closet that qualified as formal wear, except for the dresses she'd worn as a magician's assistant. Seeing how The Great Ronaldo's show had a Roaring Twenties theme, her costumes were primarily flapper dresses and chunky, strapped heels. She had brought the dress with the least number of sequins, hoping it wouldn't be too conspicuous.

Lana had spent the past hour studying the group's travel itinerary. Tomorrow looked to be a busy day. She hoped that she'd be able to recall all the details during her welcome speech. Ten minutes before the dinner officially began, Lana smoothed down her dress and made her way upstairs.

When the elevator doors opened, Lana was treated to a panoramic view of Pest. The neo-Gothic Parliament Building, with its multitude of white spires surrounding a massive red dome, dominated the waterfront. The many towers and decorative pinnacles reminded Lana of icicles. The restaurant was a large neoclassical space with arched doorways and delicate flowers molded onto the ceiling. The chandeliers were made of hundreds of crystals, glistening and twinkling as the air moved. Lana's group had a private dining room reserved towards the back. On the ceiling of their private dining hall were cherubs playing lutes, flutes, and harps for a woman in flowing robes, resting on a fluffy cloud.

Five older ladies already occupied a large circular table in the center of her group's private hall. These were the widows – and the reason Lana had to add gray highlights to her hair. She sucked up her courage and headed over to their table, a smile already planted firmly on her lips.

As she approached, Lana noticed that they all had the same short and extensively layered haircut, colored the same rusty-brown hue. *They must all use the same hairstylist,* she thought, wishing they did not. It was so much harder to tell them apart this way. And she was so bad with names, as it was. Upon closer examination, Lana realized they all were wearing comfortable pants, no-nonsense blouses, and walking shoes. Lana was certain they had all brought sturdy and practical jackets with them, as well.

"Hello, ladies, it is a pleasure to meet you. I am Lana Hansen. I'll be replacing Gerta, the guide who was hospitalized."

"Well, bless me. Dotty did send an older replacement. I told you girls she would. Dotty is always looking out for us." The speaker was a touch plumper than the rest and wearing the brightest shade of red lipstick Lana had ever seen. From her boisterous tone, she was clearly the leader of the group.

The woman's words stopped Lana in her tracks. *How old do I look?* she wondered. *I didn't put that much gray in my hair.*

The speaker must have noticed the astonishment on Lana's face. "Time ages us all differently, dear." She patted Lana's hand. "You've still got a great figure."

Lana's eyes widened in humiliation as she gulped down a snarky comeback. "Ah, thanks. I just wanted to introduce myself and see whether you needed anything before dinner is served." Lana started backing away automatically, praying more guests would arrive so she didn't have to entertain this bunch. Her ego couldn't handle many more potshots.

"Don't pay any attention to Frieda. She doesn't realize how blunt she can be. She doesn't mean any harm," the frailest-looking of the bunch responded in a gently teasing tone. A wooden walking stick leaned against her chair.

Frieda glared at her companion yet said nothing.

"It is nice to meet you, Lana. We are all glad you were able to interrupt your holiday to help us enjoy Budapest. I'm Sara. I might need your arm now and again. The streets are pretty icy, and my hip replacement surgery was only three months ago. I don't want to mess it up again."

"Of course. I'm happy to lend you a hand."

"I'm Nicole," said the shortest of the bunch as she leaned over to shake Lana's hand.

"Julia," said the woman sitting next to her, as if answering roll call.

"I'm Rebecca," said the last, "but you can call us the Fabulous Five if it's easier."

Lana choked back her shock, snorting instead.

"Bless you, Lana," Sara said.

"Though we might not be the Fabulous Five for long. Doris's husband has been in and out of the hospital all winter. When Doris joins the club, we are changing our name to the 'Sexy Six,'" Rebecca responded, her many bracelets jangling as she pounded her fist on the table.

"Nothing's been decided, Rebecca," Nicole snapped.

"All I know is that 'Fabulous Five' is far better than the 'Fetching Four.' I hated that name," Julia grumbled.

"We are so glad you joined us last year, Sara," Frieda said, patting her friend's hand.

"I enjoy traveling with you, too. I only wish that my husband's dying wasn't a prerequisite for joining this group," Sara groused.

Frieda shrugged. "Rules are rules."

"Could you send a waiter over? We'd like to eat our dinner now," Julia asked. "There's no sense in waiting on the rest. They always show up late. I swear, all we've been doing this whole tour is waiting on the others."

"No problem," Lana said, her tone self-assured as she searched in vain for a waiter. "I'll go ask one to come over and take your order. Give me a moment." Lana strode away confidently, despite the fact that she had no idea where the massive restaurant's kitchen was. She headed towards a tuxedoed man holding a tray of empty glasses.

"Could you send a waiter over to our section? My guests would like to order. I can help pour drinks, if it would speed things up."

The waiter smiled easily. "Sure, go through those double doors over there. On the right you will find someone to take your group's order." He sped off before she could thank him.

Lana did as suggested, and sure enough, she was back with a waiter and water pitcher in no time.

Another table was now occupied. It was the middle-aged couple who didn't want to be disturbed in the whirlpool. Now they were elegantly dressed, and based on the wife's snooty expression, they obviously were accustomed to being waited on.

Lana began to fill the Fabulous Five's water glasses while the waiter took their orders, when the woman from the whirlpool said, "Excuse me, we are waiting to order."

Lana groaned internally. From the haughty angle of the wife's chin, Lana knew the woman was going to be a pain in her backside on this trip. Remembering her promise to Dotty – happy clients equal five-star reviews – Lana walked over to the table with her brightest smile already in place.

"Hello and welcome to Budapest. I am Lana. I'll be helping Carl with the rest of this tour. And you are?"

"Hungry. What's taking the waiter so long?" the woman responded while flicking the folded napkin into her lap.

Her husband laughed heartily. "Don't mind my wife. It's the jet lag. We would love to see the menu." *Of course,* thought Lana, *this is Helen and Tom Roberts, Dotty's last-minute additions. The ones who received such a significant discount.*

"Great, I'll bring one over," Lana said, as she walked towards the kitchen. Helen called her back. "We want to order an *aperitif* first. That's what it means – before food." The woman's tone was the same an adult used with a small child. "You know what? It's almost New Year's Eve. Bring us a bottle of champagne."

"Of course. I'll let the waiter know. But I want to make sure you understand that only wine and beer are included in the tour price," Lana said, keeping her tone deferential.

Tom went white as Lana spoke, then raised his finger as if to protest his wife's order.

Helen clicked her tongue at her husband and locked eyes with Lana. "What are you waiting for?" she hissed.

Lana scurried off to the kitchen. She hadn't thought every guest was going to be a sweetheart, but she sure hoped the others weren't as conceited as that woman.

When the waiter brought a bottle of Budapest's finest bubbly, he made a show of popping the cork and letting Helen sniff it before pouring them both glasses. Helen seemed at ease with an expensive drink in her hand. She threw back that first glass in one gulp and signaled for the waiter to refill it. Her husband looked as if he was going to be sick.

Soon two more guests arrived, an older couple both dressed impeccably in muted greens and browns. *They must be the Hendersons*, Lana thought, veering off to shake their hands.

"Welcome to Budapest. I hope you're doing well. I'm Lana Hansen, I'll be taking Gerta's place on the tour. Can I get you anything? A drink or bread basket?"

Mrs. Henderson looked to her husband, a puzzled look on her face.

Her husband leaned into her ear and yelled, "She's the new guide. Lana."

Harold turned to Lana. "Hello, it's good to meet you. I'm Harold, and this is Margret. You'll have to excuse my wife. Her hearing aids got crushed in transit to Vienna, and we haven't been able to get them fixed. I'm afraid she can't hear well without them. You'll have to speak up when you want her to answer."

"Oh, okay, no problem, Mr. Henderson," Lana said, knowing she would never be able to address them by their first names. "Can I get you a drink, Mrs. Henderson?"

"Yes, please. Two martinis."

"Coming up," Lana said loudly while nodding and giving her two thumbs up.

"Thank you, young lady. Say, Dotty said you were able to come over and fill in at the last minute. That was sure nice of you. But doesn't your husband mind you being here, instead of with him on New Year's Eve?"

Mr. Henderson's question was innocent enough, but it felt like another gut punch. "I'm not married, so that's not an issue," she responded and started to walk away.

"It's never too late to tie the knot. We've had our share of ups and downs. But in your twilight years, you realize how important it is to have someone to love," Mr. Henderson said, then yelled into his wife's ear, "Life is better together."

Mrs. Henderson planted a wet kiss on her husband's cheek. "Darn tootin'!"

When the doors opened again, Lana hoped it was Carl coming to help. She still hadn't seen him and wasn't certain what she was supposed to say to the group. Instead, it was another guest, the skinny-dipper with long black hair.

The new guest glanced around the room, then made a beeline for the last empty table. Lana wasn't sure what to do. She assumed Carl and Sally would want to share that one. According to the seating arrangements, the woman was technically part of the old ladies' group. Yet judging from her age and clothes, the twenty-something probably wouldn't enjoy dining with them. Lana thought of asking Helen and Tom whether the latest addition could join them, but one look at the wife and Lana decided to leave them be.

Instead she walked up to the young woman. "Hi, I'm Lana. I'll be escorting the Wanderlust group for the rest of this tour. You are welcome to sit here, but there will be another couple joining you shortly. There is also a place set for you at that table," Lana said as she gestured towards the older ladies. They all waved back. "Dinner will be out shortly. Would you like a drink first? Perhaps a beer or wine?"

The young woman looked annoyed. "Is Carl here?"

"Yes," Lana said, caught off-guard. "He is still part of the tour. I'm taking Gerta's place, the guide who was hospitalized. I imagine Carl will be here shortly." At least Lana hoped he would be here soon. Where was he?

Lana had assumed he would have arrived early to dinner, as she had, to help get the guests settled. But maybe that had been Gerta's task. Dotty had made clear that Carl's primary responsibility was the logistics – getting the guests and their luggage from one location to the next – but not escorting the daily tours. That was Lana's job. The meals were a gray area they had yet to discuss.

How she wished that she and Carl could have chatted before dinner started. She had knocked on his door several times, but hadn't gotten a response. And she didn't dare knock on Sally's door. If Carl was in there, she did not want to disturb the lovebirds. Sally had arrived a few hours before Lana did, and she could imagine they would want some time alone before joining the group.

Truth be told, Lana really didn't need Carl's help right now, other than for moral support. Still, it would have been nice to chat first, as colleagues, before Lana sprung into the deep end. Dotty had given her a thick dossier containing the schedule for each day, with names and telephone numbers of the local guides and operators. She had used the same companies for the past five years running, so Lana didn't expect any hiccups. But she still wanted to confirm their tour itinerary with Carl at some point this evening.

The young woman smiled broadly. "Well, then I'll have a daiquiri."

"Okay, I'll ask the waiter to bring one over. Do you mind if I ask your name?" Lana asked.

"Jess."

"Great, I'll be right back." Lana walked to the kitchen, a puzzled frown on her face. Why the heck was this pretty young thing alone during the holidays and on a trip meant for older, rich Seattleites? When she had read that the girl's mother booked this trip as a Christmas present, she had envisioned a dowdy young thing, too shy to have found a partner to spend the holidays with. This girl looked ready to go clubbing in her skin-tight pencil skirt, spiky heels, and silver glitter top. Her sequins sparkled in the light, outshining those on Lana's dress. The girl's hair was a mass of curls and hairspray. She was a gorgeous young woman; it was only too bad about her arrogant attitude. But then, a girl who looked like that was probably used to getting what she wanted.

When Lana returned from the kitchen, daiquiri in hand, she was relieved to see Carl entering the restaurant, with Sally on his arm. Sally looked radiant in her high-collared black dress, her curly blond hair extending over her shoulders.

35

As they approached, Lana noticed that Carl's normally neatly pressed clothes were rumpled, as if he had slept in them or gotten dressed in a hurry. The skin under his left eye was a deep blue, as if he had been recently punched, though he had clearly tried to cover it up with foundation that had smeared. When she looked closer, she realized Sally's curly blonde hair was frizzier than normal and her dress's many buttons weren't done up correctly.

"Sorry we were late," Sally announced to the group with a giggle. "Carl and I had some catching up to do." Carl looked towards the ceiling.

Sally broke free from his arm and enveloped Lana in a bear hug. "Hi Lana, it's great to see you. Dotty told me you were her saving angel. I am so glad you didn't have any other plans. Otherwise poor Carl would have to do everything, and we wouldn't be able to spend so much time together!"

Lana reddened, again reminded of her status as recently single in a painful way. Sally didn't seem to notice. Instead, she released Lana and announced, "We will take a bottle of their best champagne. Carl and I have something to celebrate."

Sally thrust her left hand into Lana's face. Around her plump ring finger rested a large diamond surrounded by a plethora of tiny sparkly ones.

"Carl just proposed."

The Fabulous Five and Hendersons clapped heartily. Carl looked sheepishly around the room, nodding in response to the congratulations.

Jess threw her napkin onto her plate and stormed out of the room.

"I guess she wasn't hungry," Sally quipped, seeming to be completely unaware that her fiancé followed Jess with his eyes, a desperate, pleading look in them.

To Lana, it seemed as if Carl wanted to be anywhere but here. This was not the charismatic man she remembered from Dotty's parties. *What was going on?* Lana wondered. When she and her now ex-husband announced their engagement, they were giddy to the point of irritating others. Lana couldn't help but be curious. Investigative journalism had trained her to read people's body language and read between the lines of what they were saying. She hoped for Sally's sake it was just cold feet that Carl was experiencing.

"Congratulations, Carl." Tom raised a glass of champagne, in his honor.

Carl turned to face him, apparently noticing Tom for the first time. "What are you doing here?" Carl whispered as his face drained of color.

Helen's brow furrowed as she looked at Carl, then her husband.

"Thank you," Sally gushed, clasping her hands together. "Carl is the best thing that's ever happened to me. He's the love of my life. I feel like a princess."

"He's a real prince, alright," Tom responded with a laugh.

Helen looked at her husband as if he was crazy. "Do you know him?" she asked. Tom ignored her and polished off his champagne.

Lana showed Sally and Carl to their seats. "Thanks for coming over at such short notice, Lana," Carl said.

"No problem at all. I'm happy to help Dotty out and see Budapest. Hey, are you alright? Did you go skibobbing, too?" Lana asked, pointing at his blackened eye.

"Oh, we got a little rambunctious, and he ran into a door," Sally tittered, making Lana blush. Moments later, the waiter brought over a log-shaped pastry and set it between Sally and Carl. "For the happy couple," he said demurely.

"What the heck is that?" Sally asked.

"It is *bejgli*, a traditional Christmas treat. It's a pastry roll filled with walnut."

"Oh, I've never tasted that before." Sally took a hesitant bite. "This is scrumptious! Oh, Carl, you'll love it." She cut off a piece and pushed the fork into his mouth. He obediently chewed and murmured his approval, a strange grimace on his face. To Lana, Carl looked uncomfortable, not love-struck.

After she'd ensured that all of her guests were happy, Lana took Jess's place at the Fabulous Five's table to wait for their meal to arrive.

Moments later a team of waiters brought soup to their tables. One cleared his throat to get the group's attention. "We have two kinds of soups for you to sample tonight. The first is *halaszle*, a traditional Hungarian paprika-based fish soup. It is quite spicy, so do be careful when trying it. The second dish is *gombaleves*, a soup made from wild mushrooms and sour cream. Hungarians use the bread to soak up the broths. Enjoy."

Soon Frieda exclaimed, "Phew, that is delicious, but the peppers are setting my mouth on fire."

Lana took a tentative bite of the fish soup, feeling the burn on her tongue. It was quite spicy but not much more so than the Thai curries she loved to make back home. The fish melted in her mouth as her stomach rumbled in satisfaction.

After their plates were cleared, Lana helped refill water and wine glasses until the waiters returned with their main course – a hearty green salad and beef stew.

As the plates were served, one waiter announced, "This is goulash. It is probably Hungary's most famous dish. There are many variations; we hope you enjoy ours."

Lana poked around her bowl with a fork. It was a rich stew filled with tomatoes, carrots, onions, potatoes, paprika, and beef. Her grandmother had always made the most wonderful stews. She breathed in the peppery smells, her mouth watering in anticipation. The first bite was just like Grandma used to make. It was wonderful.

During dinner, the Fabulous Five told Lana about the group's visit to Vienna and Prague. It sounded like they'd had a wonderful Christmas and had gotten to visit many lovely markets, concerts, churches, and monuments during the first ten days of the tour. Lana also learned that the women loved to gamble and had visited several casinos along the way. Apparently Nicole was quite lucky at blackjack.

"The snow made everything seem like a fairy tale, though it was slow going on the sidewalks," Sara said. "I sure hope it won't be too icy tomorrow. I can't afford to fall again; I doubt Medicare will pay for two hip operations in one year."

"We were lucky Gerta, our first tour guide, didn't race us around the city. I hope you'll remember to take it easy, too," Frieda said, emphasizing her point with her fork.

Lana nodded solemnly. "I promise."

"Great. Now, down to business. Are you married?"

"No, not anymore. Sadly, my divorce was finalized a month ago."

"Are you kidding?" Frieda snorted. "Divorce is the best thing that ever happened to me. My husband was a domineering jerk. After we separated, I finally got to live life the way I wanted to."

Lana thought wistfully back to her married days. All nine years had been blissful. So often she had envisioned growing old with Ron. She still missed Ron's silly tricks, working together on a new act, how it felt to amaze a crowd, and even roughing it while on tour. Ron was a lot of things, but he was fun most of all.

It all happened so suddenly, she hadn't really had time to process his betrayal and give it a place in her heart. She was still reeling from his message telling her it was over. It was the last thing she'd ever expected to happen, and it felt like a punch in the gut. She trusted him implicitly, and he let her down. Perhaps if she had found him and his new assistant in bed, she could have gotten it through her thick skull that he didn't love her, that their relationship was well and truly over. But all she had was a text message and divorce papers.

"What happened?"

"He left me for his new assistant."

"Ah, yes. Why do so many men have trouble keeping their pants on? Our friend Carl appears to be one of those, as well," Frieda added, keeping her voice low this time. The tables were spaced well apart from each other, but she obviously didn't want to risk drawing Carl's attention to their conversation.

Lana was puzzled. Carl might appear a bit glum at having his wings clipped, but surely he wouldn't be getting engaged to Sally if he was interested in someone else, she thought. "What do you mean?"

"Ever since Prague, they have been an item. At least, it sure seems like they were hooking up, didn't it, girls?" Frieda looked around the table and received a wave of nods in return.

"I swear it was like watching a magnet change in polarity. The first day in Vienna, he wouldn't look her in the eye. By the time we arrived in Prague, he couldn't leave her be. It was as if he was bewitched. I don't know what that Sally woman thinks she's doing marrying him, but if I were her, I would watch out for any missteps before I tied the knot," Frieda continued. Based on her dedication to the Fabulous Five and its widow policy, Lana wondered whether she was the right person to serve as marriage counselor.

Rebecca laughed. "I think Frieda is just jealous."

"He does have a thick head of hair and is easy on the eyes," Nicole acknowledged.

"They did seem real close in Prague, I'll grant you that. But to be fair, Carl didn't accompany us on the day trips, at least not until the other guide broke her shoulder. We couldn't really observe them up close those first few days," Julia added, as if trying to temper Frieda's accusation by injecting a sense of doubt.

"Ladies, are you talking about Jess?" Lana asked, her tone incredulous.

"Jezebel, if you ask me," Rebecca said, nodding.

"That guide Gerta should have known better than to try skibobbing for the first time at sixty. My goodness, those things get up to 120 miles per hour. What did she think was going to happen?" Frieda said.

"Where's your sense of adventure gone, Frieda? I'm sure they didn't intend to crash into each other," Sarah chastised her friend. "And it sure did look like fun to me. If only I was twenty years younger."

When Frieda looked away and humphed, Sara turned to Lana. "We've been friends since grade school. I'm allowed to knock her down a notch or two."

"Wait, are you certain Carl and Jess are an item?" Lana asked, hoping to steer the conversation away from skibobbing and back to her fellow guide's cheating ways.

"As sure as I can be without sneaking into their bedroom," Frieda stated solemnly.

Lana balled her fists as a wave of anger surged through her body. How could Carl cheat on Sally like that? And with someone on the very same tour, to boot? And if he was so interested in Jess, why did he propose to Sally? It didn't make any sense. Or were the Fabulous Five just filling in the blanks with the juiciest scenario they could envision? Lana hoped that for Sally's sake, it was the latter.

She snuck a look at their table. Sally was feeding Carl bits of bread and wiping his chin. Carl looked as if he wanted to disappear from the face of the earth.

Lana looked down at her plate of goulash and told herself that it was none of her business what Carl was doing. The first night of a six-day trip was not the right time to confront Carl about his infidelity. She needed this job, and Dotty had sent her over to help keep everyone happy, not start a fight. Lana took another bite of her stew, but her emotions seemed to have wiped away her sense of taste. The delicate flavors and mouthwatering smells she'd relished moments earlier were gone. Everything tasted like cardboard.

Lana closed her eyes and exhaled, forcing evil thoughts out of her head. She was here to lead this group, not administer marital advice. When she looked around the room again, Lana realized most of her clients were finishing up their dinners. It was now or never. Lana rose and cleared her throat before addressing the small crowd.

"Welcome again to Budapest. This promises to be a wonderful week. The weather reports are positive. Yes, it is cold, and they expect occasional snow flurries, but no storms are on the horizon. We hope this will be an unforgettable experience for you all. Just as in Prague and Vienna, you will have a local guides and a bus to take you around the city. And we have our own private boat for our two-day cruise on the Danube River. It promises to be a wonderful week." Lana looked around the tables, making eye contact with the guests. Helen and Tom stared at her blankly. Sally smiled in encouragement as Carl took a large swig of beer. The Fabulous Five and the Hendersons all waited attentively for her to finish talking so they could finish their dinners.

"Tomorrow after breakfast, a local guide will lead us around Buda Palace. Afterwards, we will return to the hotel for a short break, before visiting the Christmas markets in the evening. Please be in the lobby five minutes before eleven so that we are all ready when the bus arrives. It is a three-hour guided tour of the palace, labyrinth, and Fisherman's Bastion. Light snow is expected, so please dress appropriately. If you don't want to join the entire tour, there is a café we can meet up at afterwards. I will point it out after we arrive." Lana crossed her fingers, hoping she could find it without having to ask the local guide.

"If you have any questions, please do not hesitate to ask."

"When will we have time to visit the spas?" Frieda asked.

"On December 31, you will have an entire day to pamper yourselves," Lana

41

said. There were no further questions, so she concluded, "I am in room 15 if you need me. Enjoy your dessert."

7

Room Service

Lana had just snuggled into her comfortable bed when her hotel phone rang.

Figuring it was Dotty, she answered with a sleepy hello as she turned on the lamp on the nightstand.

"The room is too cold. I want two more blankets brought to my room. Now."

"Umm, who is calling?" Lana sat up in her bed, letting the comforter slide down her pajama top.

"Helen Roberts, room 27."

"Oh, hello, Helen. Did you already call reception?"

"Why would I do that? We pay you so we don't have to deal with foreigners."

Lana stared at the receiver in shock. *What a horrible woman*, she thought. How could a human being treat another so callously?

Lana had to bite her tongue before responding. She promised Dotty five-star reviews. And Dotty had warned her that the guests would keep her on her toes.

"Okay, I'll – "

Lana heard a click, then grating beeps. She let out a growl before calling the hotel's receptionist and asking for the extra blankets to be delivered to her room.

By the time she'd splashed water on her face and pulled her clothes back on, the bellboy had arrived. She tipped him generously, then headed upstairs to room 27.

The sound of her footsteps disappeared in the plush carpet. As she approached Helen's room, she could hear shouting coming from the end of the hallway. It sounded like Tom, Helen's husband.

"Drop the act, will you? Why do you have to keep this pretense up, even on vacation?" he yelled, his frustration evident. "Nobody cares how much money you have. They're here to see Budapest. I can't take it anymore. I miss my wife. I don't like this person you've become since your father died."

"How dare you talk to me like that!"

"Helen, do you realize how badly you treat others? As if they are your servants – even the tour guides! Try treating others with respect and maybe people won't cheer when you keel over, like they did when your dear ol' pa finally bit the bullet."

Helen laughed a thin bray that traveled easily through the closed door. Lana blushed in embarrassment, wondering whether the occupants of the neighboring rooms could hear them fighting, as well.

"Really, Tom? You don't seem to mind spending Dad's money. Did you think I wouldn't notice that you'd maxed out the company credit card to book this trip? I'm the one who pays all the bills, in case you forgot. You told me you planned this long ago, but you booked it last minute, didn't you? What is going on? Why are we here?"

"To see Budapest, why else? You said you wanted to see more of the world."

"Yes, Bali, Fiji, Cape Town… but not an eastern European city in the dead of winter. Come on, Tom. We've been married too long. What aren't you telling me?"

"I need some fresh air."

"Don't you walk away – "

Lana backed three steps away from the door just as Tom opened it and stormed out. He slammed right into her, the blow cushioned by the fluffy blankets in her hands.

"Pardon me," she said, but Tom was already walking past her to the staircase at the end of the hallway.

Helen stepped into the hallway and glared at Lana. Her face was free of makeup and covered in a spiderweb of lines that somehow made her look more vulnerable.

"You took your time," she snapped, then took the blankets out of Lana's hands and slammed the door in her face.

8

Exploring Castle Hill

December 28 – Day Two of the Wanderlust Tour in Budapest

Lana greeted her guests heartily, checking to make sure everyone was happy with their breakfast. She was nervous yet excited about her new adventure as a tour guide. Her only hope was that everyone would be in a good mood. That would make the day so much more enjoyable.

So far, it wasn't looking promising. Most of the guests had trouble smiling when she greeted them. Only the Hendersons seemed bright-eyed and bushy-tailed.

Helen barely made eye contact when she demanded a cappuccino; her husband looked away when he ordered the same.

The Fabulous Five were dead quiet, and most had trouble keeping their eyes open. "Ladies, how are you doing this morning?" Lana asked.

"Alright, I guess. Though I didn't expect to lose so much at blackjack last night," Frieda said, her tone cranky.

"Yeah, well, if you had listened to me and not drawn that last card, you would have won big. But no, you never listen," Rebecca scolded.

"It's not like you did much better," Frieda grumbled.

"Three hundred euros is nothing to sneeze at," Rebecca said with a huff and turned away from her friend.

"If you could bring over a fresh pot of coffee, we would be grateful," Sara said.

"No problem, more caffeine coming up!"

When Lana turned towards the kitchen, she noticed Jess was nibbling on a croissant while staring at Carl and Sally. Carl appeared to be trying his hardest to ignore Jess completely, yet he wasn't quite succeeding. Now and again his eyes wandered over to the younger woman and seemed to get stuck there, Lana noted. "Do you need anything else, Jess?"

Jess shook her head.

"Another coffee, my love?" Sally asked Carl when Lana came over to take their order. Jess cleared her throat loudly, and Carl cringed.

Lana shook her head in disappointment. Maybe the Fabulous Five were right about him and Jess. *What was he thinking?* Lana wondered. Jess had to be half his age. The only consolation was that Sally didn't seem to notice Jess's infatuation.

Lana placed her group's order with their assigned waiter, then chugged her latte, immediately regretting it. Her tongue burned on the hot milk. She took a drink of water, holding it in her mouth to cool her tongue as she watched the waiter deliver her group's drinks.

Lana was certain things were going to come to a head when Jess knocked into Sally's chair, causing her to spill her coffee. To make matters worse, Jess rubbed her butt against Carl's arm while Sally was bent over cleaning up the spilled drink. And Carl didn't push her away.

Lana's eyes narrowed. How could Carl do that to Sally? How could he propose to her while he was clearly chasing after another? Lana raced over to help clean up the coffee, using her hip to nudge Jess aside. Jess moved on begrudgingly, her eyes never leaving Carl.

As much as Lana was looking forward to their cruise on the Danube River, she was dreading being cooped up with this bunch for two nights. She hoped they could manage to get through the meals without anyone killing another.

#

An hour later, their tour bus slipped and slid its way up the windy streets of the Castle Hill neighborhood towards Buda Palace. What Lana thought was one enormous structure was in fact a series of buildings clustered together on the tippity-top of Buda Hill. The architecture was a splendid mix of Gothic, baroque, and Renaissance. Flower beds, snow-covered this time of the year, were dotted about the complex. Lana imagined it would be even more beautiful here in the spring. Imposing statues of regal knights on armored horses and copper-topped monuments turned green from age completed the picture.

After they entered the complex, they followed the signs towards the History Museum. Carl detached himself from Sally long enough to help Lana find their local guide, a small bespectacled man in his late fifties. He bowed graciously at the group, introduced himself, then immediately launched into his well-rehearsed speech.

"Welcome to the Royal Palace. Here you can experience the splendor and glory of the Austro-Hungarian Empire and get a glimpse of the lives of the aristocracy. This palace, completed in the thirteenth century, is now recognized by UNESCO as a World Heritage site. We will start our tour by introducing you to the history of the many palaces, museums, and churches located here on top of Buda Hill. We will then visit our History Museum before walking to the upper level of the palace grounds. There we will see Matthias Church and Fisherman's Bastion. Before we begin, I do want to warn you that despite the grand exteriors, almost none of the original interior decorations or architectural details remain. In fact, most of these structures were rebuilt in their original style after the war ended. When the Nazis occupied Hungary in 1940, they used these buildings as their offices and stripped them clean. Bombs and fires during World War II destroyed the rest."

Lana could feel her group's enthusiasm waning the longer he spoke. *Great*, she thought sarcastically, *he really knows how to win a crowd*. She hoped he had a few interesting stories to tell; otherwise this was going to be one long tour.

He led them slowly through the complex of palatial buildings, most now home to history and cultural museums, pointing out the few remaining original details and explaining the castle's long and turbulent history.

Not much of a history buff, Lana did her best to listen, but in reality she was more interested in simply looking at the buildings' exteriors than in learning why or how they had been constructed.

Frieda did her best to challenge the guide's knowledge, but by the end of the first hour, even she was content to just follow along and listen. Sally had attached herself to Carl and wasn't letting go, Lana noticed. But in contrast to last night, Carl seemed happy to cuddle with her. He held her hand as he pointed to a statue or monument he liked, and she chatted easily about the paintings and costumes she admired. *Maybe I was seeing things last night and Carl truly is in love with Sally*, Lana thought, hoping for Sally's sake that she was right.

However, the snake in the grass – in the form of Jess – followed a short distance behind them, her eyes always on Carl. Several times she seemed to try to brush up against him, but each time, he eased Sally between them, causing Jess to retreat.

Oddly enough, Lana got the impression that Tom was also keeping his eye on Carl. *How did they know each other?* Lana wondered. Seattle was a village of sorts, but she doubted Carl and Tom ran in the same social circles. From what she had gathered so far, Tom worked for a yacht rental company, owned by his wife. And Helen had made clear that she saw them as above the other guests. As if to reaffirm Lana's suspicions, Helen and Tom trailed behind the group, purposefully walking a good distance behind the rest.

The Hendersons, bless them, were right at the front, keeping pace with their guide better than most of the Fabulous Five. Lana only wondered how much of their guide's lecture Mrs. Henderson could understand. Lana and Frieda took turns assisting Sara when she feared the path was too icy.

After their guide finished leading them through the last of the palace buildings, he paused at the exit and addressed the group. "We are now going to walk up to Fisherman's Bastion and Matthias Church. It is only a few minutes' walk; however, I advise you to button up your jacket. The winds are quite fierce today, especially on the upper level."

Their guide led them up the steep pathways and stairs towards the top of the hill. Luckily for Lana and her guests, someone had the foresight to sprinkle salt on the stairs and pathways; otherwise this would have been far too slippery to traverse. They soon reached a large gate and climbed another steep staircase to the top.

Lana couldn't help but shiver when the wind whipped through her jacket. The guide was right about the weather; the winds here were far stronger than she'd anticipated. Then again, they were so high up, the buildings on the Pest side of the river looked like dollhouses. She ignored the biting cold and enjoyed the views, before Helen's voice broke her concentration.

"Watch out, will you?" Helen snapped. Lana turned to see Jess had stumbled and bumped into Helen while taking a picture.

Helen turned to Jess, presumably to continue her tirade, when her features softened. "You look so familiar. Have we met before?"

Jess glared back at her. "You could say that. I've served you dozens of cappuccinos this past year. I don't recall you tipping once."

Helen's eyes went wide in recognition. "Of course! You work at the marina's café, don't you? Fancy you being on the same tour as us." Helen looked at Jess's skintight pants and stud-covered leather jacket with disdain.

"What, lowly waitresses aren't allowed to take a vacation?"

"You can do whatever you want. I just didn't expect to see someone of your age on this kind of tour. I thought someone like you would prefer to go clubbing on a beach during spring break," Helen said curtly and turned on her heel.

"People like me enjoy culture, too." Jess spat out the words, but Helen was already walking away.

Despite the obvious tension among many of the members, Lana ensured her group stayed with the guide as he led them through the upper complex of buildings. They first stopped to marvel at the flying buttresses, spires, and colorful geometric pattern of tiles decorating the roof of Matthias Church. After explaining its history, their guide pointed to a fairytale-like structure straddling the edge of the hill.

"That is Fisherman's Bastion. It was built to celebrate the thousandth birthday of the Hungarian state and finished in 1902. The unique style is inspired by early medieval architecture. From here, you have the most spectacular views of Budapest in the city."

Lana gaped at the seven white stone spires topping the series of covered passageways and balconies leading along the hill's edge. They merged together to form a path leading to a circular churchlike building constructed from the same stone.

From the passageway and open balconies, the panoramic views of the city were spectacular. Lana took in the forested hills touched with snow on the Buda side, the bridges straddling the river, the pattern of homes and streets far below, and the massive Hungarian Parliament Building on the Pest side.

"We are lucky it is not snowing today. The skies are clear," the guide said. He pointed to his left. "There you can see Margaret Island, just behind the yellow bridge named after it. If you look to your right, most of you will recognize Chain Bridge. It was completed in 1849 and was the first bridge to cross the Danube."

Lana half-listened, but was more interested in soaking up the glorious views from their high perch. A light layer of snow covered the many rooftops, though much of it had blown away in the strong winds. Her guests were busy photographing everything in sight. She felt sorry for the friends back home who would have to look through all those pictures.

"Boy, it sure is cold here. I guess I can't complain about Seattle's winters anymore, can I, Carl?" Sally said with a laugh.

"Let me warm you up, dumpling." Carl stood behind her and wrapped his arms around her torso, holding her tight. Sally snuggled into his embrace and rested her head happily on his chest. Carl kissed her head as they enjoyed the views together.

As painful as it was to be around a couple in love, Lana was glad to see them happy. She wasn't convinced that she could ever love again, though her friends firmly believed that she should get back on that horse as soon as possible. Dotty and Willow had a long list of potential dates they were dying to set her up with, but she couldn't imagine going out with anyone else. How could she ever trust a man again, after Ron had left her like that?

Lana shook her thoughts loose, focusing on the beauty of Budapest instead. Suddenly she realized that Sara was still inside the enclosed passageway, leaning heavily against the stone wall. Lana had gotten so caught up in her own thoughts, she'd forgotten about assisting the older lady.

"Can I help you?" Lana asked.

Sara looked up at her with a grateful smile. "Thanks, Lana. It does look treacherous."

"My pleasure. Oh wow, would you look at that," Lana gushed as they stepped out towards the balcony's railing. The sunlight broke through the clouds and lit up the river, making the waves in the Danube River sparkle like diamonds.

"It looks like a big fat snake slithering though the city, doesn't it?" Sara said.

Lana laughed. "It sure does have the same shape. I'm going to take a few pictures, if you don't mind."

"Be my guest. In fact, would you take one of me with Pest in the background? My daughter always complains that I forget to take selfies on my trips. She likes to travel vicariously."

"I'm happy to, Sara. I can imagine she'll appreciate seeing her mom enjoying herself abroad, more than just pictures of random buildings."

The snow made the castle, views, and Fisherman's Bastion even more enchanting than she had expected. Yet it was a struggle to stay warm. She was so glad Dotty had advised her to buy a good pair of gloves for the trip. She was especially thankful for the knitted hat and scarf that Dotty had given her. If only she had bought a warmer jacket when she was at Second Hand Love. She was shivering so badly, she figured most of her snapshots would be blurry.

Just as Lana hoped the older guests were doing okay, she overheard Frieda grumble, "Now I know what meat in a freezer feels like" to Rebecca.

Their guide must have heard her, too, because he announced, "Good news; it's time to warm up. I will now take you to the National Music Museum, then escort you back down to the entrance for the conclusion of our tour."

9

Warming up in the Café

"So, what did you like most about the tour?" Lana asked. This simple question was a psychological trick she had learned while working as a kayaking guide. Getting her clients to relive their favorite moments of the tour immediately afterwards was the best way to cement into their memory that they'd had fun. A happy customer was more likely to recommend her tours to their friends. Thanks to that little trick, she'd gotten quite a few referrals. Unfortunately for her former boss, it hadn't been enough to keep the company afloat.

Her group was inside one of the many cafés dotted around the Buda Palace complex. They were seated around a circular table positioned close to the open hearth. The fire roaring inside helped drive the cold from their bones. A glass of warm cider or hot chocolate was placed before each guest.

Frieda looked around the table, as if daring someone else to answer first. "I expected our guide to know more about the Habsburg period. But he did seem to know a lot about the Communist era," she conceded.

"I loved it," Sara said. "Walking around that palace made me feel like a princess."

"Jess, what about you? What did you like the most?" Lana asked. The girl was at least twenty years younger than all the other participants and seemed embarrassed to speak up in front of the group.

"Oh, umm, I liked the pianos."

Helen clicked her tongue in irritation.

"They are gorgeous. I love that you could listen to recordings of how they sound when played," Lana replied, smiling encouragingly. Jess's weak grin in return was a great start.

Helen tutted and let out a small sigh. Lana decided to go on the attack, in the hopes of preventing the woman's negativity from further affecting the group. "Helen and Tom, you've been pretty quiet so far. What did you think of the palace?"

At the mention of his name, Tom stopped glaring at Carl and turned to Lana. "The view of the Danube from Fisherman's Bastion is quite impressive."

Helen rolled her eyes. "She meant the palace, Tom, not the view."

As if anticipating Lana's next question, Helen added, "They could have done more to restore the interiors. I had expected them to be more lavishly decorated."

Lana's smile wavered slightly. "That's a valid point, Helen."

"What I want to know is: How did they survive without central heating? These winters are pretty cruel," Rebecca said, shivering violently for effect.

"I love those dresses. Boy, those aristocrats were tiny! I swear, I could wrap my hands around the waists, they were so small!" Sally added, her tone exuberant.

"And did you see how intricate the embroidery was? I think I would have gone blind if I'd had to do all that work," Nicole added.

"Seeing Matthias Church was worth the trip," Mr. Henderson said in a loud voice, as his wife nodded along. "It's even more beautiful than we had expected."

Lana excused herself, letting the guests swap impressions while she freshened up in the bathroom. Being a guide was a lot easier than she had expected, though her face was starting to hurt from smiling so much. She did facial stretches in the mirror until her cheek muscles relaxed, before heading back.

When she returned to their table, Lana was happy to see most of the group laughing and chatting as if they were old friends. Even Jess had joined in and was chatting easily with Tom about sailing. Lana noticed, though, that she kept one eye fixed on Carl. Several times, Jess leaned over the table and tried to engage him in conversation, but Carl only ignored her and tightened his grip on Sally's shoulder. Sally didn't seem to notice; she was having too good a time debating the merits of sleeping in a four-post bed with the Fabulous Five. Even the Hendersons appeared to be following along.

The only person who refused to join in was Helen. She leaned back in her chair with her arms crossed over her torso, a sour expression on her face. *What is that woman's problem?* Lana wondered. *How can anyone be so mad while on vacation? It's not like the trip cost them much, at least not in comparison to the rest. Why can't she just relax and enjoy herself?*

Lana sat at the end of the table, listening and laughing. When there was a lull in the conversation, she stood up to address the group. "Are we all warmed up now?"

The group nodded.

"Excellent. Our next stop is the labyrinth underneath Buda Palace."

"What do you mean, labyrinth? Is it a maze?" Sara asked.

"Not a maze, per se. It is a series of tunnels that have been used to house products, prisoners, and World War II supplies. Some say Count Dracula was also imprisoned there. There are displays inside explaining the labyrinth's history, for those who want to learn more." Lana added, worried Frieda would test her knowledge as she did their Hungarian guide. She had just shared all she could recall about their next destination.

"Sounds interesting," Sara said. "I would like to take a look." Her friends agreed.

"And if we aren't interested?" Helen asked.

Lana refused to let her drag the tour down. She turned to Helen, her smile radiant. "Anyone who would rather not visit the labyrinth is welcome to stay here and have a drink on Wanderlust Tours. We will meet here in an hour, then head back to the hotel together for a two-hour break. Tonight we will be dining at a traditional Hungarian restaurant and enjoying a tour of the Christmas markets. They are the most impressive in the evening, when the lights are on," Lana said convincingly, hoping the information Dotty gave her was still up to date. Having never seen a European Christmas market, she had no idea what to expect.

"I'm going to skip the labyrinth. I assume wine is included under 'drink'?" Helen asked.

Lana smiled tightly, unsure whether Dotty would approve. *Happy customers leave five stars*, she reminded herself. Lana doubted Helen would leave a five-star review for anything, though; the woman seemed to be able to find fault with everything and everyone.

"Of course, the first drink is on us," Lana said. "Who else would like to visit the labyrinth?"

"Not me!" Sally exclaimed. "I hate being in elevators. I don't think small places are for me."

"That's a good point. Anyone suffering from claustrophobia may want to skip it."

"I think we will enjoy the fire and a nice a hot toddy," Mr. Henderson said in a loud voice so that his wife could hear him.

She nodded in agreement. "It is rather cold out, and these chairs are so comfortable," Mrs. Henderson answered in just as loud a voice. It reminded Lana of how her own grandmother would yell unwittingly when she had her hearing aid out, simply because she couldn't hear her own voice.

"No problem. I'll send a waiter over," Lana said, not surprised they would rather sit and rest. The snow was gorgeous, but walking around in the cold air for so long had chilled them all to the bone. And the Hendersons were in their nineties.

"Carl?" Lana asked.

He shrugged nonchalantly. "Why not?"

"I'm game," Tom said. Helen looked at him, one eyebrow raised, and shook her head. *Is Helen actually forbidding her husband to join us?* Lana wondered. As if to defy her, Tom slipped his coat on. Helen looked away but said nothing. *Wow, she really keeps him on a short leash.*

Carl gave Sally one whopper of a kiss before leaving her seated next to Helen. He leaned over to Lana and whispered, "I need to visit the little boy's room first. Do you mind waiting?"

"Of course not. I'll help everyone into their jackets," she whispered back.

Sally blew butterfly kisses at Carl until he exited the room.

"Okay, folks, let's get our jackets back on before we leave. It's starting to snow again," Lana said, her voice cheery.

As Lana helped her older guests, Sally pulled out a ball of wool and two travel-sized knitting needles, then set to work. They were shorter and narrower than the needles she used at home, with a sharper point. From the looks of it, she was almost finished with a Valentine-themed dog sweater. Two terriers sat nose to nose, their muzzles resting on a giant red heart.

"That's adorable, Sally. But why does Dotty have you working on this trip?"

"She didn't ask me to do this. It's one of my new ideas. I thought I'd surprise her with it when we got back."

Helen looked over at Sally's creation and raised an eyebrow. Lana wondered what they would talk about for the next hour. She couldn't imagine that the two women had much in common. Helen, apparently having the same thought, began digging through her purse.

Tom tried to peck Helen on the cheek, but she was too busy with her search to respond. Instead, he looked at Lana expectantly.

"We need to wait for Carl, then we can walk over together," she said.

"Ah, here it is," Helen mumbled. A prescription bottle marked "Valium" was in one hand. She popped a pill into her mouth and used the rest of her cocoa to wash it down.

Lana's eye widened at her casual use of a heavy sedative. Tom stood behind his wife, absently gazing out the window at the falling snow. *Did he even notice what Helen just did?* Lana wondered. The Fabulous Five definitely did not. They were all standing with their noses pressed up to the glass, oohing and aahing at the white specks, apparently forgetting that they would soon be outside in it.

Sally smiled at Helen and asked, "What do you do, Helen?"

"I own Lake Union Yacht Rentals. It's based out of Aurora Marina," Helen responded without making eye contact.

"Oh, yeah? My yacht is docked at that very same marina. It's the one between Aurora Bridge and Gas Works Park, right?" Sally said enthusiastically.

Helen looked at Sally with interest. "Funny, I've never seen you there."

"To be honest, I hate sailing. I get so seasick. My husband used to go sailing every week. He's been dead five years, but I can't bring myself to part with his yacht. And Carl does enjoy sailing when he's in Seattle. You may know it – *If the Shoe Fits*? It's the name of his chain of footwear stores."

Helen looked up to Tom. "I don't recall, but then again, I'm not at the marina on a daily basis. That's Tom's job."

Lana followed Helen's eyes up to her husband. Tom had gone as white as a sheet. "Is *If the Shoe Fits* your yacht?" he asked, his voice a whisper.

Sally frowned. "Yes, why?"

"It's a beauty," Tom said, though his tone was anything but enchanted. He sounded distraught, or perhaps even scared. "Say, where is your fiancé?"

"Here's Carl," Lana said as her fellow tour guide rejoined the group. "Okay, gang, why don't we head out."

Lana held the door open for her guests. "Sara, let me help you. It is rather icy out." She held out her arm and let Sara grab hold, then gently propelled them back out into the blustery winter's day.

10

The Labyrinth

Carl led them through the castle's courtyards towards a broad stone staircase descending to the back of the palace. The stairs ended at a quiet street running alongside the massive foundation upon which the palace had been built. *It must be five stories tall*, Lana thought, as she looked up at the solid stone wall in wonder.

On the other side of the street, a building painted in bright yellow caught Lana's eye. Above the entrance in flashy gold letters was "House of Houdini." Lana laughed at the irony. Her ex-husband had dreamed of visiting this temple dedicated to his favorite magician for years. And now, here she was, only feet away, with absolutely no intention of stepping inside. Being surrounded by magic right now might just break her spirit.

"Enter only if you dare!" Carl said with a chuckle when they reached the entrance to the labyrinth. "Panoptikum" was etched in stone above the door. A sign hanging out into the street read "Labirintus" and was decorated with Hungarian flags. Visible just inside was a poster advertising Count Dracula's tomb.

Lana skipped to the head of the long line and gave her name, and her group was ushered inside. She could see why travelers preferred having Dotty prearrange so many aspects of these tours, and she herself was grateful that their local contacts were so well organized.

As soon as they entered, mood lighting and mist created an eerie fog slowly floating through the corridors. Most tourists were clustered near the entrance. Lana led her group further into the main tunnel, pointing out the signs that showed them where they were in the circular maze of passageways. "From what I understand, this main tunnel narrows and, at one point, there is a section with no lighting. That is intentional, so do be sure to have your phone ready."

"Why? Are we supposed to call for help when we get that far?" Sara asked.

"No, you can use its screen to light up your way. I doubt they would appreciate it if we used lighters, and I didn't bring a flashlight." Lana smiled, trying to put her guests at ease. She was so thankful that Dotty's travel notes included details such as "phones as flashlights."

"Further in, there are rooms with waxen figures dressed in opera costumes as well as a tribute to Count Dracula. Please don't freak out when you come across them."

"Did Dracula live down here?" Frieda asked, taking in the earthen walls and ceiling with wide eyes.

"From what I understand, that is an urban legend. But I bet there will be more information about his connection to the labyrinth farther in. If there are no other questions, why don't we meet by the entrance in forty minutes? That should give everyone enough time to read the information panels and explore the tunnels."

Nods of agreement all around as the Fabulous Five also took the precaution of setting stopwatches and alarms on their phones. Lana did the same, then waited to see what her group would do – split up or stay together.

Carl was the first to make his move. "I'm going to see how far this tunnel leads. See you later," he said, without waiting for anyone to answer.

"Sounds like a good idea," Tom said, and began following him. Carl glanced back in surprise, though Lana sensed irritation as well.

Seconds later, Jess also set out after Carl, but Frieda squeezed in front of her and slowed the younger woman down. "So, Jess, is it? What do you do back in Seattle?"

Jess stopped in her tracks and answered, apparently too surprised to be rude. "Me? Oh, I'm a waitress at Lake Union Café, next to the Aurora Marina."

"That sounds classy. Do you get to go sailing often?"

Jess looked towards Carl's retreating figure and smiled. "Sometimes."

"What's it like being a waitress? Do most people tip well?" Nicole asked, also steering her body in front of Jess, effectively hindering the girl's passage.

They are saving Sally's honor, Lana realized, as Julia moved in to block the younger woman on the left.

Lana figured they had the Jess situation under control. But she was still curious about Tom and what his connection to Carl could be. Every time Lana looked at Tom, he seemed to be watching Carl like a hawk. And Dotty did say he had been looking for Carl when he came into Wanderlust Tours. But why? Lana couldn't figure out how they would know each other.

Curiosity drove her down the darkened corridor, in pursuit of Carl and Tom. The poorly lit tunnel twisted left, then right, and back again. The ceiling was uneven and rocky; Lana was glad she wasn't taller. The sides seemed to narrow in sections, then widen for a few feet, before narrowing again.

Lana wasn't too keen on cramped, dark places. The only consolation was that, in comparison to the chilly winter weather outside, it was toasty warm inside. Electric torches lit the way, throwing shadows up on the walls. Information panels explaining various aspects of Budapest's history were placed throughout the maze of corridors.

Soon she came across the much-hyped exhibition dedicated to Dracula. It was a wooden coffin marked off by velvet ropes with the word "Dracula" painted on it. A small statue of a vampire dog rested on top. The thick fog combined with blue and red lights made it all rather cheesy, not as spooky as Lana imagined the exhibition makers hoped it would be.

Lana pressed on, passing a few other visitors heading back towards the entrance. The farther she went, the fewer people she came across.

She continued following the arrows pointing her forward, deep into the labyrinth. A few minutes later, Lana heard muffled voices echoing off the passageway. The longer she listened, the more it sounded like two men fighting. She moved slowly towards the raised voices until she could see Carl's backside.

"What do you mean, the work isn't scheduled? I've already given you the down payment. They should have started on the repairs by now."

"The owner's really ill and hasn't been in the office for weeks. I'm not sure when they'll be able to begin."

"If they aren't going to do the work, then I need the money back."

"Is that why you followed me all the way to Budapest?"

"Yes! You've been avoiding me for weeks, and I need to find a solution to this mess before January 15. After that, I'm sunk. If you return the money I gave you, I can at least salvage some of the fleet before we go belly up."

"About that..."

"What's your excuse this time?"

"I've been down on my luck for quite some time..."

"What are you saying?"

Carl laughed. "My poker's been off for months."

"I could kill you!"

Lana felt a surge of adrenaline. Was Carl in physical danger? Should she try to save him? She took one step forward, then stopped when she heard Carl chortle with laughter.

"Go ahead, kill me. Then you'll never get your cash back. But heck, if you spot me another five grand, I can try to jump-start my lucky streak tonight."

"Are you serious? How gullible do you think I am?"

Carl cackled, "Pretty damn gullible."

"How dare you –"

When Lana heard a scuffle ensuing, she rounded the corner while humming loudly. Carl was on his knees, and Tom's fist was frozen in midair, poised right over Carl's left eye.

"Oh, there you are," she said, pretending not to notice their brawl. "It's time to head back to the café."

The men glared at each other, then Tom released his grip on Carl's shirt and pushed past Lana.

"Everything okay, Carl?"

Carl took a deep breath and rose slowly, brushing his knees off before responding, "Yeah, everything's fine." He checked his watch. "You're right.

We should round up the group and head back to the restaurant."

11

Christmas Markets and Zither Players

Nine of the eleven members of Lana's group were sipping mulled wine in the lobby's lounge, patiently waiting for their evening to begin. They had a busy night planned: first a Christmas market, then a traditional Hungarian meal and folk music.

Sally sat between Nicole and Rebecca, chatting easily with the ladies about the morning's trip. Carl stood behind her chair, his hands on her shoulders. Jess sat alone a few tables away, looking a bit forlorn as she stared out at the snowy streets.

Helen and Tom sat at the back of the lounge. They were already on their second glass of wine. Helen was making a show of having trouble holding her glass, thanks to the oversized bandage on her finger. Sally had dropped a knitting needle at the café while waiting for the group to return from the labyrinth. Helen, shockingly, had been gracious enough to pick it up. Unfortunately for her, the travel needles were quite sharp. It was only a tiny prick, but it must have been deep because it bled enough to require a bandage.

"I'm going to check on the Hendersons," Lana said. She headed to the elevator and pushed the UP button. When the doors opened, the Hendersons were inside.

"Oh, there you are!" she exclaimed.

"I hope we haven't kept you waiting long. It took me a while to find my mittens. Lord knows it's too cold outside to go without them," Mrs. Henderson said.

Lana patted her shoulder in a reassuring way as she screamed into the woman's right ear, "It is not a problem, Mrs. Henderson. You are right on time." The woman smiled brightly.

"Are you two going to be alright tonight, Mr. Henderson? It has stopped snowing, but the sidewalks will be icy. I would be happy to take your arm, if that would help?" Lana realized her arm was already called for, but given the circumstances, she hoped Sara wouldn't mind leaning on Frieda during their walk through the market.

"That's kind of you, but we lean on each other." Mr. Henderson took his wife's arm and gently squeezed. She leaned over and pecked him on the cheek, then tittered.

Lana wanted to cry. This was how she had imagined herself and Ron in fifty years, growing old together. Instead of weeping, she smiled as radiantly as she could, though her eyes weren't in on it.

After they returned to the lounge, Lana announced, "Okay, gang, are you ready to visit one of Budapest's world-famous holiday markets? Be sure to button up. It's much colder now than it was on our day trip, but the lights should make up for it. Afterwards, we'll be able to warm up at the restaurant."

She ushered her group into the waiting bus. The driver had the heater on full blast, but Lana couldn't stop shivering. Otherwise, their ride through downtown Budapest was pleasant. The plethora of lights and holiday decorations brightened up the streets. Lana could imagine the city would be quite dreary during the winter otherwise.

They soon arrived at Vorosmarty Sqaure, their first stop in the heart of Budapest. It was the oldest and, many claimed, the most beautiful Christmas market in the city. Lana had never seen one before so she couldn't judge for herself. Regardless, it was a delight for the senses – full of color, festive lights, music, and enticing aromas. A choir of young men sung traditional songs. Their cheery melody put a spring in Lana's step as she gazed around in wonder. The smells of roasting nuts and sausages competed with the cinnamon and caramel wafting through the air. Strings of colorful lights were draped around the tree trunks and above the pathways winding through the many market stalls.

The chalet-like stands were filled with a mix of handicrafts, food, and mulled wine. Their wide, overhanging roofs were decorated with evergreen boughs, more lights, and ornaments. They reminded her of Leavenworth, a Bavarian-inspired village close to Seattle that Dotty loved to visit. Picnic benches were placed sporadically, giving patrons a chance to rest and eat. There was no shortage of food. It seemed like everywhere Lana looked, there were sausages, grilled vegetables, dumplings, candies, edible Christmas ornaments, pastries, and cakes for sale. She didn't know where to begin; everything looked delicious.

Lana chose a *kurtoskalacs*, or chimney cake, a cylindrical-shaped pastry covered in cinnamon, and nibbled at the sumptuous dessert as she trailed her guests through the busy market. Helen and Tom seemed to walk through it all without seeing, while the Hendersons took more delight in the music than shopping. Jess ordered a drink and sat next to an open fire. Sally and Carl walked arm in arm, Carl apparently content to let his fiancée lead him around.

The Fabulous Five seemed to buy something from every handicraft merchant they passed. Lana saw Sara point to a large wooden structure that resembled a three-tiered tray used for high teas. When Lana moved in closer, she realized it was a hand-carved nativity scene, spread across three circular layers of wood. The heat from candles placed on the edges of each tier powered a small rotor built into the top, which slowly turned the small figures around in a circle. Lana was as captivated as Sara, though she didn't know how the heck she would get it home. The thing must have been a foot tall.

Lana's nose drew her next door to a man serving mugs of mulled wine. He scooped the sweet drink out of an enormous ceramic pot resting on a wood-burning stove. The warm steam evaporated quickly in the icy air, and the hot liquid felt wonderful on her hands, even through her gloves.

Too soon, Carl broke free from Sally's grip and came over to her. "It's time to round up the group and return to the bus."

"Okay, I'll let everyone know."

"Great, I'll ask the bus driver to turn on the heater," Carl said.

"See you soon," Lana responded. Carl was already walking away, and Jess was right on his tail. Lana frowned and looked around for Sally, hoping she hadn't seen Jess follow him. Luckily, Sally was deep in conversation with the Fabulous Five about which Christmas ornaments they should buy next.

Lana's curiosity got the better of her. She quickly ran after Carl and Jess, eager to see how he responded to the younger woman's advances. For Sally's sake, she hoped he rejected them flat out.

As Lana pushed through the crowds in pursuit, she saw Jess catching up to Carl. She grabbed his arm just as Lana closed in on them. Lana ducked into a stall selling advent wreathes and pretended to shop.

"Carl, why are you ignoring me?" Lana could hear Jess saying. "You can't seriously want to marry Sally. Why tie yourself to that old biddy when you can be with me? After everything you told me during our last sailing trip, I know I'm the one you love!"

Lana peeked around the corner and saw Jess was kissing him passionately on the lips.

Carl returned the kiss, then leaned his forehead against hers. "It's complicated, Jess. I've got no choice but to marry her."

"You always have a choice. Who do you really want to spend the rest of your life with?" Jess moved in to kiss him again, but Carl pulled away and grumbled something Lana couldn't hear.

"When you come to your senses, you know where to find me," Jess said, then sauntered back towards the group, shaking her hips as she went. Carl watched her walk away, then slunk off towards the bus.

Lana stepped further into the market stall so that her body was partially camouflaged by Christmas decorations. She breathed a sigh of relief after Jess passed her by without seeming to notice her.

Lana stared unseeing at the bright colors and delightful designs, her thoughts turning dark. How dare Carl cheat on Sally, and so blatantly? Her first instinct was to tell Sally everything. Yet when she walked back to the group and saw how Sally was laughing along with the Fabulous Five, oblivious to her fiancé's deception, Lana stopped in her tracks. She couldn't be the one to break Sally's heart.

Truth be told, if one of her friends had warned her about Ron and his new assistant, Lana doubted she would have believed them. She had been too much in love with Ron to accept that he would be capable of deceiving her in that way. *Stay out of it, Sally is not your friend,* Lana told herself. If it became too much of an emotional burden, she could always talk to Dotty about it. She and Sally were good friends, and Dotty had a way of making even the worst news sound like a blessing.

Right now, her focus needed to be on getting her guests to their next stop. Lana quickly found Tom, Helen, and the Hendersons and led them back to the bus, before returning for the rest. The Fabulous Five and Sally were just where she'd left them, at the Christmas ornament stand. The Hungarians were famous for their intricately decorated cookies, meant to be hung on the tree and eaten on Christmas Day. "Okay, ladies. Are we ready to go?"

"Just about, I have to pay for this second bag," Nicole said.

"They sure are delicious," Frieda mumbled, her mouth full of cookie.

"I thought you were buying those for your nieces."

"These are too good to save. I can always bake up a batch of gingerbread cookies when I get home."

"Heck, save yourself the trouble and tell them they all broke in transit," Rebecca said.

Nicole rejoined the group, a large bag of cookie ornaments in hand. "I'm ready. You lead the way, Lana."

Lana spotted Jess sitting by the fire, polishing off a shot of brandy. "It's time to go," she called out, not really caring whether Jess joined them. Right now, she would be happy if the younger woman somehow missed the bus. Unfortunately for Lana, she rose and followed the group. Soon they were all in the warm bus and on their way to dinner.

Minutes later, she and Carl were ushering their group into a small café-like restaurant with long tables and padded benches. After getting them settled around one close to a low podium in the center of the dining room, Carl saddled up to her and whispered, "We usually help serve the drinks and appetizers here. That way they can get on with the cooking. It's a small, family-owned restaurant, and they appreciate the assistance." He led her to the tiny kitchen where platters full of glasses, water pitchers, and wine were ready to be served.

"Of course," Lana said, without looking at him. As much as she wanted to confront Carl, she knew it was not her place to do so. Instead, she picked up a tray of glasses with one hand and a pitcher with the other. As she poured drinks for her guests, Lana noticed Helen and Tom were actually participating in the group's rehashing of the day's events. And they even seemed positive. Perhaps simply sitting at the same table was all it took for them to join in the group spirit.

Appetizers soon filled their table. The large plates of cheese, sausages, pickled vegetables, and breads were quickly consumed. It was salty, hearty, and heavenly. Lana hopped about, helping to serve drinks and answer her guests' questions about tomorrow's tour of Pest, the concert at the Saint Stephen's Basilica, and their cruise on the Danube River.

Once all of her guests' needs were satisfied, Lana enjoyed the rich food, washing it down with a large glass of locally made red wine.

Their savory meal was accompanied by a zither player specializing in classic Hungarian folk music. The young man's instrument reminded Lana of a guitar without the long neck, yet this one had many more strings. Its surface was lacquered black with a rose painted on it. It lay on a small podium in front of the musician, who used his fingers and a pick to play it. The strings were so close together that every note sounded like a chord. Lana thought the melody was enchanting, but the Fabulous Five didn't seem to care for it. Sally nuzzled up against Carl and tapped her foot in rhythm, clearly enjoying the music. Tom and Helen even seemed to be swaying in time with the beat. Jess appeared too drunk to care.

Too soon, Carl left to find the tour bus and make certain the heater was on. Sally looked so forlorn without him. Lana sat down next to her. "How are you doing?"

"Wonderful. It's a dream, being here. Dotty was so kind to set this up. I don't know what I would have done without Carl this holiday. Christmas was bad enough, but nothing is worse than being alone on New Year's Eve."

Lana thought of her empty Seattle apartment. "Yes, if you are in a relationship, it's important to be together," she said, keeping her tone even.

"Especially when it's true love," Sally responded quickly, oblivious to Lana's comment or single status. "And I know that Carl is the one for me. I can't wait to start planning our wedding as soon as we're home."

Lana bit her tongue and stared at the zither player.

12

A Nose for Sleuthing

"Phew, what a day," Lana said aloud, then felt foolish. Seymour wasn't here to listen to her moan. With a few exceptions, the evening had gone swimmingly, but Lana was wiped out from her first full day on the job. The Christmas market was more expansive than she had imagined. She closed her eyes and recalled the classic music filling the air, the colorful ornaments, and the delicious scents. The dinner was also a success. Before Carl returned to collect them, the zither player was joined by a violist, and soon Frieda and Rebecca were dancing on their chairs in time with the lively Hungarian song.

This was far from her first time leading a tour. Back in Seattle, she had taken tourists for two- to five-hour trips around Lake Union, through the Ballard Locks, and out to the Puget Sound. Yet being "on" all day, and with the same group for so long, was exhausting. She hoped that she could handle staying positive for four more days.

Lana lay back on her bed and closed her eyes. During those kayaking tours, Lana often got glimpses into her clients' lives simply by listening to their conversations and reading their body language. What she remembered most was how travel tended to highlight any tension within a relationship or group. That was certainly the case on this trip.

To keep her mind occupied during the long paddles, Lana used to make up stories in her head about her clients' lives and connections to each other. On a rare occasion, she had searched online to find out more about her clients, to see whether they matched her expectations. They usually did.

That natural curiosity had lent itself perfectly to investigative journalism. If only her source had dared to come forward, then she would still be doing what she loved most. The whistleblower was concerned for his safety, and rightfully so. The information he had smuggled out of his workplace showed how a wood-processing plant intentionally dumped chemicals into local rivers. Fifteen years later, the local salmon population still had not recovered.

Because her source refused to go on public record, the company's lawyers made mincemeat of Lana's story and evidence, easily winning the libel lawsuit they'd filed against the *Seattle Chronicle*, Lana, and her editor. Lana never did discover how much the *Seattle Chronicle* had to pay, but she and her editor lost their jobs shortly after. The company dumping chemicals got off scot-free. It made her sick to her stomach, but without her source to back up her story, there was nothing she could do.

In spite of all of that, though, her curiosity was a switch she couldn't turn off. How did Jess and Carl know each other? Lana couldn't imagine he and the young woman had met at the beginning of this tour, as Carl claimed. Jess seemed downright obsessed with him. And what about Tom and Carl? They obviously knew each other, but it sounded like a business relationship gone sour.

Lana pulled out her smartphone and searched the internet for information about Lake Union Yacht Rentals. On the "About Us" page, Tom Roberts was listed as the manager and Helen the owner. A short paragraph recounted how the company was founded by Helen's father in 1948 and began with a fleet of three boats. Their fleet now boasted fifty-seven dinghies, catamarans, sailboats, and yachts in various sizes. She scanned the boats' names, mostly puns or references to sunsets. When Lana searched online for more information about the larger yachts in their fleet, their current value appeared on the screen. Lana whistled under her breath. Several were worth a half-million dollars apiece. The company must be worth a fortune, or at least its fleet was.

Curious to see where exactly they were moored, Lana searched for the Lake Union Marina and immediately found hundreds of photos of sleek yachts, shiny sailboats, and well-maintained tugboats. In the search results, a recent news article with the headline "Local Marinas Victim of Storm Mary" caught her eye. Lana recalled that a series of vicious storms had caused all sorts of damage on the islands in the Puget Sound, as well as the Seattle waterfront. When she clicked on the link, the lengthy article recounted the destruction, focusing on the damage done to boats moored at several local marinas, including the Lake Union Marina. The photos of the damage would make any sailor howl. Masts were snapped in half, and several yachts were lying on their sides, partially filled with water. Lana slowly scrolled through the pictures, paying attention to the names of the damaged vessels. She maneuvered back to the Lake Union Yacht Rentals fleet list. By golly, her eyes weren't deceiving her; several of Helen's rentals had been damaged during the storm. That might explain why booking this trip had maxed out the company credit card. But if they were in financial trouble, why on earth had they decided to come here for a holiday? Even with the discount, Wanderlust Tours' trips were absurdly expensive.

Lana pondered these facts, realizing if the boats had been damaged in a storm, the insurance should have covered the repair costs. Why would Carl be involved in getting Tom's fleet repaired? Carl was a gambling-addicted tour guide, not a boat mechanic. Whatever it was, it sounded like Tom hadn't told his wife about it. Otherwise he wouldn't have been desperate enough to follow Carl to Budapest.

Unable to find any more clues as to Carl and Tom's relationship, Lana moved on to Jess. What was she doing on this tour? She obviously had little interest in Budapest or travel. The only things she cared about were Carl and posting selfies on social media. Lana smiled, knowing where to look to find out more about Jess. She clicked on Instagram and found ten names that matched her guest. Soon enough, she found Jess's profile.

There were hundreds of selfies, yet only a handful featuring another person. Unfortunately for Sally, the other person was Carl. Lana clicked on the most recent, a sunset shot of Jess and Carl on the deck of a boat. In the background was the Seattle skyline. Carl was kissing her cheek. Behind them was a wooden plaque with the name of the boat on it. "If the S..." was all Lana could make out. The caption read: "Spending time with my man." It was posted six weeks ago, right before Carl left for Europe to lead three tours in a row.

Lana wanted to scream in frustration. Sally's yacht was called *If the Shoe Fits*. It was too much of a coincidence to think Carl was on any other yacht. He had been taking his girlfriend-on-the-side out for trips on Sally's own boat.

Thankfully Sally was not active on social media, otherwise she might just poke Carl and Jess's eyes out with her knitting needles. How could Carl do this to her? Lana knew she had no other choice but to tell Dotty, the next time they talked. She would want to know what Carl was doing to Sally, her good friend and business partner.

As much as she wanted to kiss Seymour goodnight, she couldn't face having that conversation with Dotty right now. Lana knew she would blame herself for introducing them, as well as sending Sally to Budapest.

Lana looked at the clock and was shocked to see it was already midnight. Tomorrow her group would take a tour of central Budapest, before boarding a riverboat and embarking on a two-day cruise. She would need her wits about her. It was time to stop investigating and get some rest.

Lana turned off the light and mulled over her guests' backgrounds and connections until her eyes drooped shut.

13

Man Overboard!

December 29 – Day Three of the Wanderlust Tour in Budapest, Hungary

Lana ran her hand over the shiny brass railings as she walked up the gangplank of the *MS Franz Liszt*. The riverboat's dark wood paneling glistened in the late afternoon sun. Life buoys, decorative oars, and long poles with metal hooks were mounted to the exterior walls. Around the base of the boat hung decorative fishing nets, and at the back was a tiny lifeboat.

The ship's first mate welcomed them heartily on board, then led her group up a flight of metal stairs and into a well-lit hallway running down the center of the second floor. The boat was refitted to accommodate twenty-four passengers, but Dotty had reserved the entire boat for her group. The first mate showed each of her guests to their assigned cabins. Lana's was next to the hallway door, meaning she only had one set of clients as neighbors. Unfortunately for her, they were Tom and Helen Roberts.

Lana's stateroom was big enough to hold a queen-sized bed, two chairs, and a small table. She was surprised to see that her window was actually a sliding glass door opening onto a private balcony. As soon as she opened it, snowflakes flew inside. Lana quickly closed the door and rubbed her arms warm before unpacking her bags.

Once finished, Lana threw herself onto the bed and relaxed into the thick comforter. Now that her group was on board and getting settled in their rooms, the rest of the evening should be easy. It has been a whirlwind of a day. After a three-hour bus tour through Budapest and an afternoon concert at Saint Stephen's Basilica, her group had been given an hour to pack up their suitcases before meeting in the lobby. Lana was glad she had packed light. The ability to gather her things quickly had given her a chance to finally talk to Carl, tour guide to tour guide. Luckily, she'd learned that there wasn't much more expected of her than she was already doing. Keeping the guests happy was truly her top priority.

Lana glanced at her wristwatch and frowned. Their dinner and the evening cruise along the Danube didn't start for an hour, but she had already announced cocktails beforehand. She wanted to be the first one upstairs so she could start serving drinks as her guests arrived. The boat was small enough – and their schedule busy enough – that Dotty found it cheaper to just buy out the bar and let her guests drink whatever they fancied, instead of paying for a full-time barkeeper.

She forced her body off the bed and changed into a forest green skirt and gray sweater before heading back out. On her way to the lounge, Lana decided to quickly explore her surroundings, in case any of the guests asked about the amenities on board. The *MS Franz Liszt* was not large and thus quite cozy. Their rooms were all on the second deck of the three-story ship, with a spacious dining room and lounge on the third deck. Both the restaurant and lounge offered spectacular views through floor-to-ceiling windows. Lana was glad they wouldn't have to go up onto the upper deck to enjoy the views. In the summer, she could imagine it would be filled with lounging sunbathers. But now it was far too cold to be up there for any length of time. The smokers in her group would have no choice. To appease the nicotine addicts, there was a plastic tent set up at the back of the upper deck with ashtrays set out on two tables. Lana would have to mention its presence to the smokers in the group. So far she had noticed Carl, Jess, Helen, and Tom sneaking cigarettes whenever they were outside.

On the lowest deck were the engine room, kitchen, and staff quarters. Hanging off a small balcony above the boat's propellers were a lifeboat and fishing nets. Her stomach grumbling in anticipation, Lana wondered whether they would eat any fresh fish. She loved seafood and was spoiled for choice in Seattle.

When she heard voices on the staircase, Lana sped back up to the lounge, just in time to see her guests arriving via the other entrance.

Soon they were all assembled in the lounge, most of the guests seated on the plush cushions lining the windows, enjoying the views as they sipped their cocktails. Random bursts of fireworks exploded over the Danube River, set off by locals incapable of waiting until the new year officially began. After they moved next door to the dining room, a dancer performed for them until their food was served. After she had departed, they set sail down the Danube. Dinner was a delicious mix of traditional and contemporary Hungarian dishes that were rich and satisfying. To Lana's astonishment, almost all included paprika – even the dessert.

More than the food, Lana loved watching the skyline of Budapest, illuminated by seemingly millions of twinkling yellow lights and a hazy white moon. The grandiose architecture seemed even more beautiful at night.

The only blemish on the otherwise perfect evening was Jess. During the meal, she sat across from Carl and Sally, despite Frieda's attempts to block her from reaching the seat in time. It seemed to Lana that Jess used every excuse possible to brush up against Carl's hands, arms, and legs.

At one point, Lana felt compelled to step in by trying to draw the woman into a conversation. Unfortunately when Lana asked Jess which neighborhood she lived in, the young woman responded with, "Why do you care, Nancy Drew?" then ignored her.

To her credit, Sally pretended not to notice Jess's attention-seeking moves the first few times they happened, but at some point, enough was enough.

Before Lana could think up a way to defuse the situation, Sally exploded. "That's it! You've been flirting shamelessly with my fiancé since I got here. I'm sick of it! Stay away from my man, you hussy!"

Sally sprung out of her chair and threw her wine into Jess's face. Lana's jaw dropped in shock. Little old Sally actually stood up for herself! As the group's guide, she knew that she should scold Sally, but all she wanted to do was cheer.

Jess, however, was not about to let bygones be bygones. "Carl, are you going to let her treat me like dirt? Stand up for me, you buffoon. I am carrying your child."

The room went silent so fast it was as if everyone froze simultaneously. Lana swore she could hear a pin drop. Carl stood wide-eyed and gaping, but no words came out to comfort his fiancée. Sally was the first to make a move, running screaming out of the room.

"You've gone too far, Jess. You shouldn't have said that." Carl shook his head as he growled at her, then stormed out after Sally.

"Sally, it's not true. She's just trying to..." They could all hear him pleading as he raced down the stairs after her.

All sat stock-still on their chairs as they listened to Carl pounding on Sally's door. *Oh God,* Lana thought, *this is a nightmare.* Dotty had been right; this cruise was cursed! Carl's hammering became more intense and his tone more desperate. Lana knew she couldn't leave Sally alone with him right now.

"I'll be right back," Lana said as she raced down the stairs. Carl was much bigger than she was, and there was no way she would be able to physically restrain him. She only hoped he would have enough sense not to lash out and hurt either her or Sally.

As Lana reached the hallway, she saw that Carl's fist was in midair and the door to Sally's room was opening. Lana stopped where she was and waited, hoping the couple could resolve their dispute peacefully. As soon as Sally was visible, Carl dropped his hand and hung his head.

"You said you wanted to be with me. That's the only reason I bailed you out again. How long have you been with her?" Sally demanded.

"Dumpling, please let me explain." He looked down the corridor to Lana. "In private."

Sally stuck her head out and saw Lana. Black rivers of mascara streamed down her face. "It's okay, Lana. I'll scream if I need you," Sally said, her voice weary.

Sally stepped aside so Carl could enter, then closed the door.

Lana was torn. Part of her wanted to leave them alone, but her gut told her that things could get uglier before they improved. She stood her ground, waiting to see what happened next. She couldn't hear exactly what they were saying to each other, but from Carl's pleading tone, it wasn't going well.

Too soon, Carl's explanations were drowned out by Sally's response.

"I've wasted so much time and money on you. Here – gamble this away!" Lana heard Sally yell. Seconds later, there was a large splash.

"Sally, are you okay?" Lana tried the door, but it was locked. She pushed her ear to the door, yelling, "Sally, tell me what's happening! Did he hurt you?"

"I pushed him in, Lana," Sally called out through the closed door. She responded so calmly, Lana almost didn't believe her ears.

"Oh God, what did you do? The water's got to be freezing. Help!" Lana screamed as she ran down the hallway and back outside. "Man overboard!"

Lana raced down to the lowest deck and searched the water from the railing. The sun was down, and the metal was ice cold. She could only imagine what the water felt like. She heard Carl splashing and sputtering before she saw him a few feet from the bow.

When she looked around for assistance, she noticed a life buoy tied to the railing. Lana flung it into the water and missed. Luckily, a crew member had better aim. Carl slipped it over his head and held on tight as he was lifted back on board. The first mate covered him with a blanket, then helped him inside. As soon as they'd reached their staff quarters, the first mate said, "You need to remove your clothes and wrap yourself in dry blankets."

Carl tried, but he was shaking so badly, he couldn't get a grip on his clothes. "Let me help you, baby," Jess said in a soothing voice as she tried to break through the barrier of crew members to reach him.

Lana tugged on her arm, pulling her away. "You've done enough. Please go to your cabin before anything else happens."

Jess jutted out her chin and started to respond. The look in Lana's eyes stopped her midbreath, and she quietly did as she was told.

Two crew members quickly stripped Carl down to his underwear and then covered him with a multitude of blankets.

Soon another crew member sporting a medical bag arrived to check Carl's vital signs, the captain on his heels.

"This man could have been killed! How did this happen?" the captain asked.

Lana started to respond when Sally spoke up. The crowd of crew members parted so that Sally could approach the captain.

"He told me he didn't lo..." Sally started to explain, but was too overcome with emotion to continue. Instead, she hung her head in shame. "I didn't mean to push him."

The captain frowned at Sally then looked to Carl. "Do you wish to press charges?"

Carl turned to Sally, glaring at her as he considered his options. After a long silence, he said, "No, not at this time."

"I'm so sorry," Sally muttered as she tried to touch his arm.

"Stay away from me! You tried to kill me!"

"No, I didn't mean to..." Sally snuggled close, attempting to smother him with kisses and apologies.

Carl pushed her away. "You devil woman, I said leave me alone or I will press charges!"

Lana took Sally by the shoulders and navigated her back to her stateroom. She was inconsolable. Lana didn't know what she could say that might stop the tears streaming down Sally's face.

"I want to be alone," Sally said between sobs.

"I understand. Is there anything I can do for you?"

Sally tried wiping her eyes dry, but it was a losing battle. "I can feel a nasty migraine coming on. Could you get my medicine from the bathroom? It's the prescription bottle on the counter."

"Sure." Lana grabbed the bottle and poured a glass of water.

"Thanks," Sally said, the word getting caught in her throat. After swallowing the pills with half the glass of water, she threw herself onto her bed and began weeping uncontrollably.

Lana backed out of the room, recalling her own reaction to Ron's breakup message. It was about the same. Sally didn't need a stranger trying to comfort her, just time to let her heart accept Carl's rejection and heal.

After she closed Sally's door, Lana went to check on the others. When she returned to the lounge, Lana was surprised to see all of the other guests were sitting at one table, deep in conversation. *Nothing like a drama to bring a group together*, she thought.

Frieda pounced as soon as Lana was within earshot. "You were the first one outside, Lana. Did you see what happened?"

"Carl followed Sally to her room. They fought, and Sally accidentally shoved him into river. But Carl will be fine; the crew got him out in time," Lana said in her most reassuring voice, hoping to defuse any wild rumors with the truth.

"I'm not surprised Sally pushed that parasite into the Danube. From what she told me, he's been sponging off of her for months," Helen said.

Tom went pale and took a swig of his drink. Helen didn't notice, but Lana did. What exactly were Tom and Carl up to? And did it have anything to do with Lake Union Yacht Rentals? Lana still couldn't wrap her brain around why Tom would have given Carl any amount of money to invest. He was a part-time guide with a gambling problem, not a businessman. Nothing made sense.

"Well, that's enough drama for us. We're heading to the casino." Rebecca announced as the Fabulous Five stood to leave.

"Blackjack table, here I come!" Sara rubbed her hands together and shot Lana a winning smile.

"Best of luck, ladies. Break a leg."

"Hey, don't say that. Our bones are brittle enough that it's easily within the realm of possibilities. And we aren't performing on stage. We're going to clean out the Tropicana Casino." Nicole cackled in delight.

Lana helped the five friends hail a taxi from the dock, then returned to the lounge, secretly hoping the rest of her group had gone off to their cabins.

When she climbed the staircase to the lounge, she noticed the Hendersons were heading down the hallway to their stateroom. There was hope she might be able to enjoy a glass of wine in peace. Unfortunately for Lana, Tom was at the bar pouring two glasses of white wine. When he took them to his table, Lana poured herself a glass of red and sat far away from Tom and Helen. Lana put her feet up just as Helen's phone rang, shattering the silence.

Helen glanced at the number and muttered, "That's odd, why would our accountant be calling?" before answering it. "Hello, Samuel." She listened a moment, then exploded in anger. "What do you mean there are problems with the refinancing? Can you speak up, Sam? This connection is terrible." Her brow furrowed, and she stood up, pushing a finger into her free ear. The soft music piped into the lounge was apparently too much extra noise for her to hear properly.

She held the phone to her chest and said to Tom, "I'll be right back. I better see what he wants."

Tom stood and grabbed her arm. "What refinancing?"

"The interest rates are so low, I am refinancing the mortgage on our home."

"Why didn't you consult me first?"

Helen jerked her arm free. "Because the house is mine, isn't it? I am the one who bought it, and I am the one paying the bills." Helen turned and stalked off towards the dining room. "Let me get to a quieter place, Sam."

Tom's eyes widened as he watched his wife walk away, leaving her wine untouched. As if in a daze, he rose and returned to the bar to pour himself a double shot of vodka. He stared at it a moment, then downed it in one gulp.

Sensing another marital argument coming on, Lana decided to call it a night before Helen returned. "Boy, it's been one heck of an evening. I'm going to turn in. If you need me, I'll be in cabin 7." She picked up her wine and carefully made her way to the door.

Tom waved a hand in response before pouring another double.

Lana shook her head and sighed as she headed downstairs to her room. *Being alone is preferable to being in a relationship with such a high-strung partner,* she thought.

14

Carl, Where Are You?

December 30 – Day Four of the Wanderlust Tour in Budapest, Hungary

Lana woke up groggy and stiff. The nightstand lamp was still on, and a paperback mystery novel lay open on the pillow next to her. It had taken several chapters before she fell into a deep sleep. The boat creaked and groaned as it bobbed in the cold water. Her room was close to the main entrance, meaning she'd heard the heavy door to the hallway opening and shutting as her tour guests returned from their night on the town. Helen and Tom's whopper of an argument, audible through the thin walls, hadn't helped with her insomnia, either. More splashes, thumps, and laughter had also traveled into her room via her balcony. At one point, she'd sworn someone was knocking on the hull. Yet no one would have been stupid enough to go swimming in this icy cold water, and at night no less.

With great difficulty, Lana rose out of her comfortable bed and took a hot shower. At least she didn't have to do much today besides keep the peace during breakfast. At 6 a.m., their boat had set sail for Visegrád, a small village in the Danube Bend known for its castle, fruit brandy, and spectacular views over the river. It was a three-and-a-half-hour ride from Budapest, meaning they should be arriving shortly after breakfast. Their tour guide would meet them at the local marina to take them by taxi to Visegrád Castle, followed by a traditional lunch and a brandy tasting.

After they returned, their riverboat would travel on to the picturesque village of Zebegény and dock there for the night. Tomorrow morning they would sail back through the Danube Bend to Budapest, stopping off at the colorful village of Szentendre along the way. Dotty said this two-day trip to the smaller villages upstream was the highlight of the tour. Lana couldn't wait to tag along.

Lana opened the door to the dining room with trepidation, afraid to see who was awake and what everyone's mood was.

The Fabulous Five were polishing off their first round of eggs, bacon, and toast. "Well, speak of the devil. How did you sleep, Lana?"

"Like a baby," she said as she crossed over to their table. "And did Lady Luck smile on you last night?"

"She sure did," Frieda said, her tone satisfied. "All of us ended up leaving with more money than we came in with. I don't think that's ever happened before. Rebecca even won a slot machine jackpot!"

"I've never seen so many coins in my life! It's only too bad they were fifty-cent pieces and not those two-euro coins," Rebecca grumbled.

"It was a waterfall of money," Sara laughed.

"Wow, I wish I'd seen that," Lana said.

"And we got quite the show, thanks to Carl," Nicole added.

Lana's smile froze. "Do you mean, Sally pushing him into the Danube?"

"No, he showed up at the casino about an hour after we arrived. When he tried to enter, one of the bouncers asked whether he had another Rolex to trade in. Isn't that a funny way to greet someone? I swear, humor has changed since I was a girl."

"They held him back from entering until he pulled out a wad of cash. They didn't make us show them our money at the door," Frieda said.

"That does sound strange, though you ladies have far more experience than I do." Lana had, in fact, never set foot in a casino and didn't know the first thing about gambling.

"We were all settled into a good game of blackjack when Carl started playing poker at a table close to ours. I swear, that man is a magnet for trouble! First Jess shows up and screams at him for not taking care of their baby, then

Helen gets him kicked out of the casino. That man has no luck with women."

"Wait, what do you mean, Helen got him kicked out? And what did Jess say?"

Frieda leaned back and folded her hands over her plump torso. "Jess was berating him for not making her an honest woman, seeing as she was carrying his child."

Lana's eyebrows shot up. "I thought she was bluffing about being pregnant. How did Carl react?"

"It was the darndest thing. He just laughed at her and kept playing his game. When she tried to pull the cards out of his hand, a security guard came over and escorted her away. You should have seen the evil glare Jess shot him. If looks could kill!"

Lana couldn't believe Jess was so smitten with Carl that she would track him down at the casino. Sure, Carl was charismatic and good looking, but he was twice her age and heavily in debt. What did Jess see in him? Could she really be pregnant? Lana thought back to her first night in Budapest and how she'd seen Jess skinny-dipping in the pool. The young woman looked like she was made of skin and bones, not a mother-to-be.

"I tell you what, if that girl is pregnant, I'll eat my scarf," said Julia. "I haven't seen her get nauseated once, not even when they tried to feed us that spicy cabbage dish. The smell alone would have driven me to the toilet."

"I never did get morning sickness. But I did have to go to the bathroom every five minutes," Sara chimed in.

"I sat next to Jess on the tour bus, and she reeked of cigarette smoke. And she does love to drink daiquiris. I sure hope she's not pregnant because she might mess up her baby," Nicole added.

"Whether she's pregnant or not doesn't matter right now. We were telling Lana about last night, remember?" Frieda asked, chastising her friends for dawdling off-topic. "After Jess left, everything settled back down to normal. After Nicole won two hands of blackjack in a row, Helen showed up and then all hell broke loose. Excuse my French," Frieda said, apologizing to her crowd. "What she was ranting and raving about I certainly do not know; she was screeching so badly it was impossible to understand her."

"All I could make out was 'insurance,'" Sara added.

"And that 'she wasn't as stupid as her husband.' Boy, they must have a wonderful marriage," Rebecca quipped.

"I had just been dealt an ace of spades and was about to yell blackjack when Helen clawed at Carl's face," Nicole said.

"Then she pushed Carl into the table, and all the chips got mixed up. She's got some temper on her," Frieda interjected.

"The security guards had enough," Nicole resumed. "They kicked them both out of the casino. Carl got really mad because he was on a winning streak. I swear it looked like he was going to punch her."

"Helen? Or Jess?"

"Helen, dear. Try and keep up," Sara said.

"Good Lord, what skeletons does Carl have in his closet? It seems like every woman on the tour wants to kill him!" Lana exclaimed.

"Well, not us, or Mrs. Henderson."

"Sorry, you're right." What exactly was Carl up to? Was he having an affair with Helen, as well? Lana couldn't believe it. Helen reminded her of a tarantula, the kind that eats her partner after mating.

"When you returned to the boat, did you see any of the other guests?"

"There was someone smoking on the upper deck. I could see their cigarette butt burning. It looked like Jess to me, but then again, it was dark. I can't be certain it was her," Sara said.

Lana nodded absently. "I wonder where Carl slept last night."

"You mean with Sally or Jess?" Frieda asked.

Just at that moment, Sally entered the lounge. Her hair was frazzled and her clothes hastily thrown on. Lana could imagine she'd had a rough night.

Sally approached the table with her head down. "Hi, Lana," she said. "Carl didn't come back to my cabin last night, and he's not answering his door. I just want to make sure he's alright, but I don't want to interrupt him if he's with *her*."

Lana nodded in understanding. "I'll knock on Jess's door. Why don't you stay here?" Sally nodded, and they switched places.

Lana went down to their rooms. Jess answered on the first knock.

"What do you want?" Jess snarled at her.

"I am just trying to find Carl. Is he in there with you?"

"No, he's not." Jess slammed the door before Lana could ask to see inside. Unsure what to do next, she tried Carl's door. Her knocks became more insistent, but she couldn't hear any movement inside. She jiggled the handle, but it was locked.

After locating the first mate and explaining the situation, he opened Carl's cabin door for Lana. The bed hadn't been slept in, and there was no sign that Carl had spent time inside since they had arrived.

"If he's not here, and not in any of the other cabins, where else could he be?" Lana asked.

"We will search through the crew's quarters and engine room. But we cannot open the other guests' staterooms without their consent. Have you checked the upper deck?"

Lana shook her head, feeling foolish. Carl might be enjoying a smoke while watching the river. She could imagine he would rather not see Jess, Helen, or Sally right now. "I should have before calling you."

"It's alright. Why don't we walk up together?"

The sun was shining brightly, though the air was still crisp. Carl was nowhere to be seen. Lana looked down over the railing into the dark blue waters of the Danube. Clumps of ice rolled over the waves.

They looked inside the plastic enclosure and saw the ashtray was overflowing with cigarette butts. Several had the distinctive purple tinge of Helen's lipstick. Yet that was not what caught their attention. One cigarette had left a trail of ash, as if someone had lit it then let it burn down to the butt. It was Carl's preferred brand. Next to the ashtray was a half glass of beer.

"That's odd. It's almost as if someone was interrupted while having a drink and a smoke," Lana said.

The first mate agreed. "I will have our men search the ship and let you know if we find anything."

"Great, I appreciate it. I'll ask my guests when they saw Carl last," Lana said, her eyes never leaving the half-finished beer. *Carl, where are you?*

15

That's the Girl!

When Lana returned to the dining room, she was pleased to see that all of her guests were present. Jess sat alone at a table facing the window, an untouched croissant on her plate. The Hendersons were seated close to the Fabulous Five. The widowed friends were all smothering Sally with empathy and affection. Lana hoped it would be enough to pull her through this horribly tough time. At least her ex-husband had shown the decency to split up with her as soon as he found another, instead of waiting until she discovered he had a lover.

Tom and Helen were seated at a table for two. Lana headed over to them.

"Helen, Tom, hello. I apologize for being so abrupt, but have you seen Carl this morning?"

Tom shook his head. "No, we took our time getting dressed and just arrived for breakfast," he said, his tone brighter and cheerier than usual.

Helen looked straight ahead, almost as if she was in a daze. In contrast to every other morning so far on the tour, she wasn't wearing any makeup or flashy jewelry. She looked older and frailer without it. Based on the bags under her eyes, Helen had not gotten much sleep either. Lana wasn't surprised; she'd heard the couple arguing in their cabin before she'd dozed off. Considering they had fought almost every night of the trip, it wasn't anything noteworthy. However, in light of the Fabulous Five's recounting of their gambling night, Lana was curious as to what last night's marital row was all about and whether it had anything to do with Carl. Had Tom really given Carl money, and had Helen's accountant told her about it last night? Whatever had driven Helen to the casino, Lana was certain, Carl had not provided Helen with the answer she'd demanded.

"When did you see him last?"

Tom made a show of thinking, finally saying, "It must have been when he stormed off the boat. Helen and I were returning to our cabin from the lounge and passed him as he left. We went to bed directly afterwards. Isn't that right, Helen?"

Helen twitched at the mention of her name. *What's wrong with her?* Lana wondered. "Yes, that's right," Helen responded, still not making eye contact with either Lana or her husband.

"But didn't..." Lana started to contradict her story and ask about the casino, but she didn't dare do so in front of Tom. Whatever was going on between them, Lana didn't want to make it worse. For all she knew, Helen and Carl were having an affair, as well. Or worse, the Fabulous Five's cataracts were so bad that they confused Helen for another floozy.

Where was Carl? Between Sally, Jess, and Helen, Lana could imagine that Carl didn't want to come back and sleep on the boat. She truly hoped he had stayed the night in Budapest. But the cigarette and the half-finished beer said otherwise. And why didn't Carl think to call her, if only out of professional courtesy?

"That's the girl who was making all that ruckus last night!" Margret Henderson exclaimed in a whisper so loud everyone in the room could hear. Lana looked over to see who Margret was referring to, but her husband was lowering her pointed finger. "Shh, you're shouting again."

Margret blushed and looked away in embarrassment. Lana couldn't tell who her target was, but she seemed to be glaring at Jess. Though realistically, the way they were seated, it could have been Helen or Sally, as well. And when you were ninety, Lana figured, all three qualified as "girl."

Harold cleared his throat and looked sheepishly at the group. "You'll have to excuse us. We had trouble falling asleep last night. I know Margret is as deaf as a doorknob, but she's quite sensitive to vibrations, and the doors tremor when they close. All the comings and goings last night kept us awake."

"It's no bother, Mr. Henderson. I agree, this boat is a lot creakier and noisier than I had expected," Lana said. "By the way, when did you or your wife last see Carl?"

"After he was rescued from the Danube. I don't recall seeing him after that. We were tired, so we had hot toddies in our room before going to bed," Harold said.

Lana considered yelling the same question to Mrs. Henderson, but figured she wouldn't have seen anything different. The Hendersons were together constantly. Instead, she walked to the front of the dining room to address the group.

"May I have everyone's attention? Our guide Carl is missing. Last night was a bit unusual. He may have stayed in Budapest for the night. We are about to dock in Visegrád. A local guide will meet us at the marina and lead you on a five-hour tour of the local sights and a *pálinka* maker. That's a fruit brandy and the Hungarian national drink. I am certain you will be in good hands. If no one minds, I would like to stay on the boat and help the crew locate Carl."

"Don't we pay you to accompany us on these trips?" Helen asked. Lana wished she could give it a rest, for once.

"I guess you do. However this has been one heck of a strange turn of events. I really do need to get in touch with the owner of Wanderlust Tours and let her know what is happening, as well as try to locate Carl. I truly hope no one else will feel inconvenienced if I stay on board."

"Of course not, you've got enough on your hands, and these local guides are top-notch. I'm certain we'll be fine," Frieda said in her booming voice, in a tone that made clear what she thought of Helen.

"Thank you, I really do appreciate your help. And I know you will have a wonderful day. Enjoy your breakfast. I'll let you know when the guide is here."

16

Sally Confesses

Lana turned to walk back down to the crew's quarters when Sally jumped out of her chair and motioned for her to follow her into the lounge.

"Lana, the girls told me they saw Carl at the casino last night. I was shocked they let him in. He told me he got that black eye from a man at the Tropicana that he owed money to. What if he got himself into more trouble?"

"I thought you said he ran into a door."

Sally looked down at the floor. "Yeah, well, neither of us wanted to admit the truth."

"We should tell the captain about this. He can inform the police and have them ask around at the casino."

"No! Please don't tell the police."

"Sally, what is going on?"

"When I arrived in Budapest, Carl told me that he'd been gambling again. The night before I arrived, he lost a bunch of money that he'd borrowed from the wrong people. Some Hungarian gangster was threatening to cut off his finger if he didn't cough up another ten grand! They'd already taken the Rolex I gave Carl for his birthday, but that wasn't enough to cover his debt."

"Ten thousand dollars? Sally, that's a lot of money!"

"You're right, ten thousand was more than he usually asked for. To be honest, if he didn't have that black eye, I wouldn't have believed him. Though it wouldn't be the first time he tried to cheat someone and got caught. Carl loves to see how far he can push people."

"What were you fighting about before he fell overboard?"

Sally looked away. "He told me that he didn't want to marry me. I gave him that ten thousand on the condition that we get engaged. To be honest, I was already planning on proposing to him; I even brought the rings with me. But I wasn't certain he would say yes. When he asked for the money, I figured it was the perfect way for both of us to get what we wanted."

Lana sat next to Sally and wrapped an arm around her shoulder. "Sally, why do you..." Lana couldn't bring herself to finish the question.

"Let Carl walk all over me? I honestly don't know. I have a habit of attracting leeches – attractive ones, though. Even you'll have to admit that. And I'm not the prettiest of the bunch. I know without my healthy bank account I wouldn't be able to get anyone like Carl to even look at me. And to his credit, he can be so sweet and attentive. I just wish his love didn't come with a price tag."

"Not all guys salivate over bank accounts."

Sally snorted. "Honey, the ones I attract do."

"You know, Dotty has a list of Seattle's most eligible bachelors memorized. Trust me, I know from personal experience. Say the word and I'm certain she'll find you someone who will treat you like a queen for a change." Lana squeezed her shoulder.

Sally tried to grin, but it came out a grimace. "Thank you, Lana. You're probably right. Dotty never did like me dating Carl, but she was too much of a friend to forbid me from going out with him. Wait, if you're so certain she can help, why are you still alone?"

Lana shrugged. "I'm not over my ex yet. I guess it's easier to give advice than to take it."

17

Bringing Dotty Up To Speed

The crew's search of the boat's interior brought them no joy. Lana gazed out at the snow-covered hills and distant mountains, wondering where the heck Carl could be. Despite the problems he clearly had with several women on this tour, Lana figured his loyalty to Dotty would win out. If he hadn't contacted her, maybe he had gotten in touch with Dotty.

Lana knew she had to call her boss and tell her the bad news. She was not looking forward to that conversation. But she needed to know whether Carl had been in touch, as well as how she should proceed with the tour if he remained MIA.

They had three more days before the group flew back to Seattle, and Lana was certain Dotty wouldn't be able to send a replacement guide to help her. Would she be willing to cancel the last three days? Lana doubted it, unless there was absolutely no other option. But could she really keep the tour going on her own? The thought sent shivers down her spine.

With much trepidation, Lana dialed Dotty's number, hoping she wouldn't mind being woken up so early. Soon her landlord's sleepy voice came on the line.

"Good morning, Lana. Is everything okay?"

"Hi, Dotty. No, it's not. Carl is missing, and I don't know whether to cancel the rest of the tour or keep going as planned," Lana moaned into the phone.

"The tour must go on, Lana. Our clients have paid for three more days of travel, and by golly that's what they'll get."

Lana was silent, petrified by the thought of carrying on by herself. Yet realistically, she could handle everything on her own, as long as her group cut her a little slack. Whether Jess or Helen would do so remained to be seen.

"Lana, are you still there? I know I am asking a lot, but I've never had to cancel a tour, and I would rather not start now."

"Okay, I think it will all work out. The group will be busy with day trips until we fly back. And most of the guests are pretty easygoing. I can't guarantee five-star reviews, though."

"Oh, don't you worry about that. Now back to Carl. What do you mean, he's missing? Did he go off on a gambling binge? I thought Sally would keep a better eye on him."

"There were mitigating circumstances, in the form of a twenty-four-year-old waitress who apparently has a serious crush on Carl."

"Oh Lord, did that girl Jessica pull the wool over my eyes? I couldn't figure out for the life of me why a woman her age would want to go to eastern Europe for Christmas, all alone. Now we know."

"Unfortunately, Sally knows, too."

"Oh God, could it get any worse?"

A knock on Lana's door made her jump.

"Can you hang on one second? It might be the crew with news about Carl."

The captain stood outside her cabin door, his hat over his heart. "I am sorry to inform you that we have found Carl's body."

18

New Experiences

"I'm sorry, Captain, I don't know what 'aft' or 'starboard' means." Lana tried to focus on the man's words, instead of Carl's corpse, but she was having trouble processing her thoughts.

After his men had pulled Carl up on to the deck, they had moved him to their quarters – out of the guests' sight – and called the police in Budapest.

Lana had never been in the same room with a newly deceased body, and it was more disturbing than she had imagined. How could this person, so full of life mere hours ago, now lie dead before her? She tried to look at Carl, but his body was so discolored, she couldn't make herself look for long.

"One of my men was checking the lifeboat when he noticed a shoe caught up in a fishing net hanging on the backside of the ship," the captain explained patiently. "The shoe was on Carl's foot, meaning his head was submerged. Even if he had been alive when he hit the water, he would have only had a few minutes to get himself out. And being tangled up in that net would have made it near impossible, especially when hypothermia began to set in."

The left side of his shoulder and head were bashed in because his body had been bumping up against the hull all night, according to the captain. *That's what the thumping noise was*, Lana thought as she closed her eyes and let out a cleansing breath, forcing the nausea down. The last thing she wanted to do was puke on Carl's corpse.

"Do you think he accidentally fell overboard?"

The captain gazed at the body on the ground before him. "Yes, I do. He was the last passenger on board. My men pulled up the gangplank as soon as he'd returned, just after two in the morning. If he was already inebriated, then went upstairs to have more alcohol and a cigarette, it is entirely possible he decided to take a look at the water and fell over the railing. It has happened before, but never with fatal consequences."

Lana considered the captain's words. The railings were low enough that he could have accidentally fallen in. The views from the open deck were much more impressive than from inside the plastic enclosure. And in a drunken state, he would have been less aware of the biting cold.

"The police know your group is out on a tour, but they ask that we return to Budapest as soon as they are back on board so they can question everyone about Carl's movements last night."

"I understand. I'll inform the owner of Wanderlust Tours and the guests."

19

Fruit Brandy and Gold-diggers

When her group returned from Visegrád, giddy from the fruit brandy tasting, Lana ushered them into the lounge. The look on her face sobered them all up in a jiffy. The Hendersons and Jess sat at one table; Sally was sandwiched between the Fabulous Five on the other side of the room. Tom and Helen sat at a table smack dab between them. Lana had placed carafes of herbal tea and coffee on each table, along with a plate of Hungarian cookies, in hopes of softening the blow.

"I'm not going to beat around the bush – Carl's body has been found. It appears he fell overboard late last night, got tangled up in a net, and drowned. We are going to have to cancel the rest of the riverboat cruise and head back to Budapest. The captain said the police will want to question us all before we can disembark."

"Why do the police want to talk with us?" Helen asked.

"From what the captain told me, it's standard procedure. They'll probably want to know when you saw Carl last, that kind of thing."

Helen pursed her lips and leaned back in her chair, suddenly lost in thought.

A heart-wrenching moan escaped Sally's lips, tearing at Lana's soul. Carl had possessed quite a few horrible traits, but Sally clearly loved him. Lana had informed her of his death before the group returned. Sally's response had been intense, and Lana figured it would take her weeks to get past this pain. She was glad Frieda and Sara were back on board and could help take care of her.

"You killed him, didn't you!" Jess sprung out of her chair, almost hitting Mrs. Henderson in the process as she raced over to Sally. "You knew he was planning on marrying me and tried cutting in line by giving him that fancy ring."

"We've been dating for almost a year! You're the jezebel in this scenario, not me!" Sally yelled back. "I'm not blind. I saw you making googly eyes at Carl every chance you got, but I thought he had the sense to stay away."

"How dare you! We were in love. He was going to marry me, not you. He said so the last time he was back in Seattle. That's why he changed his will."

"Wait – you met him before you came on this tour?" Sally crumpled in her chair.

Jess, sensing the change, leaned in closer. "Yeah, we spent most of our time sailing. There's not much to do on board except explore each other's..."

"Stop!" Sally screamed, throwing her hands over her ears. "What will are you talking about?"

"Carl changed his will, leaving me his yacht and tour company."

"*His* yacht and company?" Sally's hysterical laughter filled the lounge. "Why would Carl need a last will and testament? He had nothing to leave. *If the Shoe Fits* is mine. And he's not the owner of Wanderlust Tours; he's one of the guides. Carl didn't have two pennies to rub together."

"I don't believe you! You're just trying to get me to back down so you can run off with what's mine!"

"And you are a foolish gold-digger who didn't do her homework!"

"Tom, you know that Carl was a businessman. Tell them about your deal," Jess said.

Tom looked shocked to be dragged into this conversation. "What deal? I never met Carl before this trip."

"Don't lie! I've seen you two holed up in the corner of Lake Union Café, reviewing those maintenance contracts. I know you two were in business together."

"You what?" Helen said, glaring at her husband.

Tom shook his head vehemently. "Young lady, you are clearly mistaken. I never met Carl before arriving in Budapest."

"Why are you lying?" Jess shrieked.

Why indeed, Lana thought. Tom remained steadfast that he and Carl had never met before the trip. Yet based on the conversation she had overhead in the labyrinth, they knew each other quite well. But how could she ask him about it without revealing that she'd been eavesdropping?

"It wouldn't be the first time Carl conned somebody. He probably lied about making you his beneficiary so you would stop pestering him to marry you. And it gave him a free pass to get into your pants," Sally said, her tone as bitter as acid.

"Why you – " Jess lunged at Sally. Tom sprung forward and wrapped the younger woman up in a bear hug. Frieda rushed to Sally's side, blocking Jess's kicking legs with a chair.

"Why don't you go to your cabin and cool off," Lana said to Jess. "We'll be back in Budapest within the hour."

"You've not heard the last of me. I am going to get to the bottom of this, even if I have to hire a team of lawyers! We'll see who's right once we get back to Seattle. I know Carl was telling me the truth. He never lied to me," Jess said. She elbowed Tom in the ribs. "Let go of me!" As soon as Tom released his grip, Jess stormed out of the lounge.

"I think I'm going to go lie down," Sally said.

"That sounds like a good idea. Tell you what, Lana, why don't I sit with Sally for a while?" Frieda said as she took Sally's arm and helped her stand. Sally seemed to have aged a decade within a few minutes' time. Tears flowed freely down her plump cheeks.

"Thanks, Frieda, I appreciate it." Lana hoped that Jess would have the sense to leave Sally alone. Frieda would see that she did; of that, Lana was certain.

20

An Afternoon Drink

Lana left the lounge to check in with the captain, confirming the entire group was on board and that they would soon be back in Budapest. The police were waiting for them at their dock, ready to board and interview everyone – including the crew. Though it was pretty obvious Carl had fallen overboard, it was standard procedure to question everyone, before the tour could continue on to the next hotel.

What a way to start off a new job, Lana thought as she climbed the staircase back towards the lounge. Was the tour cursed, as Dotty claimed it was, or was Lana causing this streak of bad luck? True, the guide and two guests had been injured before she arrived, but no one had actually died until she joined the tour.

When she returned to the lounge, the remnants of her group were sitting at one table and chatting easily. Tom was pouring shots of *pálinka* for the group, and Helen was serving them fruit juice to wash it down. Based on their reddening cheeks and boisterous laughter, it looked as if her group was enjoying the fruit brandy. *What is going on here?* Lana had only been gone for twenty minutes or so, yet all of a sudden her clients appeared to be getting along better than they'd had since she joined the tour. Maybe it was the brush with death. Or the generous shots that Tom was pouring. *Be grateful for small blessings*, she thought.

"Do you want a drink? We bought more bottles of *pálinka* than we're allowed to take back. Would you prefer apricot or chocolate?" Tom asked.

"Wow, that's really kind of you, Tom," Lana said, truly surprised by his generosity.

Tom shrugged, a goofy smile on his face. "Helen figured this was a good time to share it with the rest. Carl's death was quite a shock." Helen's back went stiff at the mention of her name, but she didn't turn around and acknowledge her husband. "This lot complained about it being too strong on its own, hence the juice." Tom chattered merrily away as if they were good friends.

Lana was caught off-guard by his openness and helpfulness. Tom had a new spring in his step that she hadn't noticed before they left for Visegrád. He seemed to be firmly under Helen's thumb for most of the trip thus far, but now glimpses of his own personality were shining through. He wasn't as much of a jerk as she'd thought. If only he would stop lying about his relationship with Carl.

Lana glanced over at his wife, silently refreshing the Hendersons' drinks. As Helen turned back to the bar, Lana noticed a vacant look in her eye. *What the heck happened in Visegrád to make Helen so docile?* Lana wondered.

The Fabulous Five were giggling and laughing like schoolgirls. From the looks of it, they'd already had several shots during the short time Lana was away.

"No thanks, Tom," Lana said. "I appreciate the offer, but I need to touch base with my boss first. I'll take you up on your offer after I'm done."

"Don't take too long – the brandy might be gone," he called after her.

Lana stopped at the door and turned back to her clients. "I hope you'll all be sober enough to talk to the police after we dock," she said, mildly concerned the older passengers might pass out before they arrived back in Budapest.

As if on cue, Mrs. Henderson yawned loudly. Lana couldn't blame the older lady; this tour was far more exciting than advertised, and not in a good way.

"Pardon me. I'm feeling quite tired. Between this morning's tour and this horrible news about Carl's death, I guess I'm pooped out. How are you feeling, Harold?"

101

"I could use a short nap. That *pálinka* has quite a kick, doesn't it? Lana, would you mind if we rested in our cabin until the police arrive?" Mr. Henderson asked.

"Of course not. You aren't required to stay here until we dock in Budapest. Take some time to enjoy the views or catch up on a good book. After the police are finished with us, a bus will take us to our hotel. It looks like a wonderful place to stay. And don't forget about the traditional folk dancing performance after dinner. It's still going to be a great night!"

21

A Killer on the Loose

"Lana, are you in there? You have to help me!" A muffled voice called through Lana's cabin door.

Lana blinked her eyes, adjusting to the dim light. With the curtains closed, the room was quite dark. She had tried to call Dotty as soon as she returned to her cabin, but her boss was out. So she had taken a short nap instead, after asking the captain to fetch her as soon as they were back in Budapest. But this was not the captain or first mate. "Mr. Henderson, is that you?"

"It's Margret. She won't wake up."

Oh, no, not another one. Lana thought as she threw on a bathrobe and ran out into the hallway.

Two doors down, Margret Henderson lay in her bed, peaceful yet cold. Mr. Henderson was right; she was gone. "I am so sorry," Lana whispered.

Mr. Henderson held his beloved wife's hand to his forehead, choking back tears as he searched for any sign of life in her face. There were none to be found.

"I'll go get the captain," Lana said, gently patting his shoulder. As she closed the door, Harold burst into tears, the sobs catching in his throat and racking his body.

Lana wiped at her watering eyes as she headed downstairs to deliver the bad news to the captain.

Two investigators from the Budapest police force stood inside the riverboat's lounge, notebooks open as they asked about Carl's last night on earth. Around one circular table sat Lana's entire group. Sally and Jess were locked in a glaring contest.

"Sally killed Carl and Mrs. Henderson, I'm certain of it!" the younger woman shrieked. "When Carl refused to marry her, she killed him to keep him away from me. Then she tried to poison me! Sally is pure evil."

"This is ridiculous…" Sally began, but her heart wasn't in it. Lana was shocked by how bad Sally looked. Since Carl's body had been found, she was a shell of a woman, broken and unable to defend herself. Lana's heart went out to her.

"Officer, why are you letting –" Lana said, in an attempt to cut off Jess's accusatory rants.

The police investigator motioned for her to be silent. "Miss, you will have your say in a moment."

He turned his attention back to Jess, but was clearly having trouble following the young woman's line of thinking. "How would Sally have killed Margret Henderson – or Carl, for that matter? And why? If she poisoned you, why is Margret Henderson dead?"

"That's what I'm trying to say – that jealous cow meant to kill *me*. She thinks I seduced her boyfriend, when really it was the other way around," Jess smirked at Sally as she spoke. Sally looked like Jess had plunged a dagger into her stomach. "I bet she poisoned my drink and poor Mrs. Henderson drank it instead. Sally was the first one in the lounge when we got back from Visegrád. And she's the only one with a motive to hurt Carl and me."

"And this motive would be?" The detective sighed as he spoke, obviously ready to end this conversation. Luckily for Sally, he didn't seem to think that Jess's outburst was anything more than a squabble between guests.

"If she doesn't get rid of me before we get back to Seattle, she'll lose everything. Carl left the yacht, tour company, and bank accounts to me – not her. And I have proof. You have to arrest her before she kills me!"

Lana was shocked by Jess's intensity. She was convinced that Sally was a killer. How could that sweet lady kill anyone? Lana refused to believe it, just as she refused to believe that Carl was secretly wealthy.

Sally began to laugh manically. "What money? You are out of your mind! Carl didn't own anything. Why do you keep insisting that he did?"

"I wouldn't blame you for bashing the cheating bastard's head in," Helen piped up, as if she was being helpful. The police investigators were writing every word down.

"Jess, sit down. Helen, that's enough," Lana said sternly, unable to keep her mouth shut any longer. Sally didn't deserve this haranguing, especially not in front of the police. "Nobody killed anyone," she continued firmly. "Carl fell over the railing, probably after having one too many drinks. And Mrs. Henderson died in her sleep. Screaming about murder is not helping anyone, Jess. The police just want to know when you saw Carl last."

At that moment, the lounge door opened, and an officer pulled one of the investigators aside. They spoke in hushed Hungarian before turning to face the small crowd. The investigator looked quite somber as he announced, "My team has found blood on a rescue hook. I am afraid this is a murder investigation. I will need to speak to all of you individually."

"Aw, nuts," Lana mumbled. Dotty was not going to be happy to hear this.

Lana escorted her group back downstairs to their cabins where they were to wait until the police were ready to speak to them. The investigators interviewed her first, but Lana had little to tell. She had slept poorly and heard all sorts of noises the night Carl died, but didn't know which sounds had traveled across the river versus coming from her passengers.

Within ten minutes, Lana was back in her room. After contacting their hotel and letting them know they would be checking in later than planned, she lay down on her bed and stared out the window. The sun was starting to set over the hills of Buda, casting a warm glow over the city center. The holiday lights, so festive and twinkly, grew brighter as the sky darkened.

Enjoy it while you can, she told herself, well aware that the chances of Dotty ever asking her to lead a group again were nonexistent. Why would she? Lana figured two dead bodies and a police investigation within three days' time must be some sort of Wanderlust Tours record.

Lana looked at her watch and noticed the police had been questioning her guests for almost an hour. She sure hoped they would hurry up. After the police left, they would have to hotfoot it to the hotel so they wouldn't miss their dinner and dance performance. Lana picked up the stack of information Dotty had given her about tonight's events, when heart-wrenching screams caused her to drop the pile. The papers scattered across the room as Lana tore up the stairs to the lounge and the source of the noise.

She pushed open the lounge doors and saw two police officers attempting to pull Sally's arms behind her back. A detective had Jess in a bear hug, apparently to prevent her from attacking Sally.

"Carl can't be the father. He had a vasectomy years ago! She's lying about being pregnant, just like she's lying about Carl's new will!" Sally yelled as the two policemen finally managed to handcuff her wrists.

"Why should we believe you? You obviously didn't know him that well. We've been together for seven months," Jess retorted.

"Jess must be setting me up. I don't know what happened to those pills. Lana, thank God you're here. Call Dotty and get me a lawyer!" Sally screamed when she noticed Lana's presence.

"You deserve to be locked up, you murderer! Why can't you accept that he didn't love you? You took my Carl away from me," Jess cried. Lana could see crocodile tears already forming.

Sally hung her head, allowing the police to lead her away without further protest.

"Sally, don't worry, I'll call Dotty right now," Lana shouted. The lead investigator held her back so the officers could get Sally down the gangplank and into a patrol car.

After Sally was in the backseat, Lana turned to Jess and noticed the younger woman had a smartphone in her hand. An image filled the screen, though from where she was standing, Lana couldn't tell what it was. Luckily for her, Jess was in a gloating mood.

"I found a photo of Carl's will. It's right there in black and white how I stand to inherit his boat, company, and bank accounts." Jess looked triumphant.

Lana wanted to smack her. "Sally must have been targeting me, not Mrs. Henderson. If she doesn't get rid of me before we get back to Seattle, she'll lose everything."

Lana put a hand on the lead investigator's arm, stopping him from getting into a second police car. "Please, this has to be a mistake. You can't arrest Sally on the basis of this fake will. Sally didn't kill anyone! I'm sure of it."

The officer flicked at her arm as if it was an irritating fly, then smiled condescendingly. "While searching Sally's cabin, we also found prescription sleeping pills. They were phenobarbital, a strong barbiturate. She claims it's for migraines, but it's also a powerful sedative."

"So? I bet most of the guests take sleeping pills."

"You're right. Helen also has a prescription for Valium. However, there is one difference. Sally's prescription is new, yet the bottle is almost empty."

"But Carl fell overboard, he wasn't poisoned. And Sally knows better than anyone that Carl was lying about being rich. Heck, the boat he supposedly left Jess is owned by Sally! Sally had no reason to want to harm Jess," Lana protested, wondering whether that was entirely true. What else had the police discovered about her clients?

As the investigator opened the patrol car's door, Lana cried, "Wait, did Sally tell you about the Hungarian gangster that was threatening Carl? Maybe he snuck on board and killed him before we set sail for Visegrád! Shouldn't you get all of your facts straight before making an arrest?"

The detective's face hardened to stone. "You're right; it is important to get all of the facts straight before taking a suspect in for questioning. Incredibly, we were able to piece together what happened without your help. Carl's head was bashed in with a wooden pole before he went overboard. The boat's only security camera is focused on the gangplank, and we have confirmed that no one got off or on the boat after it was raised. Considering the gangplank was raised right after Carl boarded, it must have been one of you who assaulted him, not this mysterious Hungarian gangster. One Sally cannot describe because she's never met or seen him. Did Carl tell you about this man?"

Lana looked sheepish as she shook her head.

"It seems odd to me that Carl would be threatened by a local gangster and not tell his fellow guide about it, if only out of fear for your group's safety. It appears that you know this Sally person quite well and your feelings towards her are coloring your reading of the situation. In light of the information Jess has provided about Carl's will and his public rejection of Sally, it is quite feasible that Sally wished to get revenge on both her fiancé and his mistress. Until the autopsy is complete, we won't be able to determine whether Margret Henderson was poisoned or died from natural causes. And if she was poisoned, I want to make sure our poisoner is locked up. If not, we will release your guest from our custody, with our deepest apologies."

"You can't just take Jess's word for it that Carl was rich. I don't know anything about this will, but I do know that Carl is definitely not the owner of Wanderlust Tours. He is simply one of the guides."

"I have no intention at taking anyone at their word. As soon as I am able, I will instruct our team to investigate all of Jess's and Sally's claims. Considering Sally is the one with a bottle of medicine in her possession, she is the one I will be taking in for further questioning." The investigator opened the patrol door and began stepping inside.

"But why do you have to –" Lana began to protest, but was cut off.

The investigator whipped around and asked, "Do you have any factual information to add that will help explain either Carl's accident or Mrs. Henderson's passing?"

Lana gritted her teeth, wanting to regurgitate every bit of gossip she'd heard on this trip. Yet all of it was secondhand information, and the original sources had already been interviewed. As much as she wanted to implicate Helen, Tom, or Jess, she couldn't shift the blame to another just to help set her friend free. She wouldn't be able to live with herself if she did. Lana shook her head and let the officer leave.

22

Comforting Mr. Henderson

Lana walked back to her cabin, feeling defeated. She would have to call Dotty straightaway and see about getting Sally a lawyer. Afterwards, she needed to get her group onto the bus and over to their new hotel.

A stretcher was in the hallway, and two paramedics were placing Mrs. Henderson's corpse on it, now wrapped inside a black body bag. Lana sighed, saddened by the sight.

Mr. Henderson's door was open. He sat on the corner of his bed, a gray sock in one hand and a brown one in the other.

Lana knocked on the door. "Mr. Henderson, are you okay?"

He didn't look at her, but kept his gaze fixed on the two socks. "Margret has been my rock for sixty-seven years. It may sound old-fashioned to you, but she chose my clothes for me. She always had more fashion sense than I did. What do I do now? I don't even know what socks to wear. Which pair do you think Margret would approve of?"

Lana sat down next to the elderly gentleman. "I think she would prefer you wear the brown ones. They complement your sweater."

Mr. Henderson nodded and slowly pulled on the socks and his footwear.

"Can I call someone for you? Do you have children or siblings?" Lana asked.

"The police called my son for me. An embassy worker will help him arrange a flight over. I can't leave Margret here in Budapest all alone."

"I'm glad to hear it."

The paramedics knocked lightly on the door. "Mr. Henderson, would you like to ride with your wife?"

"Yes, please."

As Lana watched the paramedics wheel Margret away, all she could think was, *and then there were eight…*

23

Causing a Heap of Trouble

"There is no way on God's green earth that Sally killed anyone, let alone Carl. What kinds of drugs are those Hungarians smoking? Is medical marijuana legal there, too?"

"Not that I know of, Dotty," Lana said. Her normally serene landlord was livid. Through her phone's tiny screen, Lana could see Dotty pacing around her living room, making tight circles on her oriental rug. The pets had enough sense to stay on the perimeter. Seymour had jumped up on top of the couch and was watching Dotty move through his half-closed eyes. Chipper and Rodney both lay with their muzzles on their outstretched legs, waiting for her to calm down enough to pet them.

"Someone else on that trip must have done it. You used to be a journalist, you have to investigate this! Didn't you win some fancy award for proving a young man didn't kill that police officer? Work your magic for Sally! Sorry, I didn't mean to reference your ex-husband. You know what I mean – find out who really did it before poor Sally spends the rest of her natural days in an eastern European prison! It's too late to save Carl. But you have to bring Sally home."

"I don't know, Dotty. The police interviewed everyone after they realized Carl was murdered. As much as I want to believe Sally is innocent, there isn't anyone else who would have had a reason to kill him."

"Bull honkey. It breaks my heart to hear that Carl had a wandering eye, but

Sally was no killer. Someone must be lying. Or that Hungarian gangster did sneak onto the boat and hurt Carl. But I know in my heart that Sally never could have done this."

Dotty and Sally had been friends for ages. Lana didn't know Sally nearly as well, of course, but had talked to her several times at Dotty's place, especially after the two ladies started up Doggone Gorgeous and Purrfect Fit. She was one of the nicest, kindest people Lana had ever met. Which was probably why other people tended to walk all over her. Sally didn't seem to have a mean bone in her whole body.

Perhaps that was the problem. Didn't they say that serial killers were often docile people who snapped? Maybe this whole business with Jess pushed Sally over the edge. But could she really have killed Carl? She did push him off the boat and did nothing to help rescue him. If Lana hadn't heard Carl floundering, he would have died during his first dip in the Danube. So what was preventing Sally from pushing him in again?

As Lana thought back to how Sally had resisted those two officers trying to handcuff her, she realized the older lady was probably more capable than she let on.

But if it wasn't Sally, who else could it be?

Jess was a home-wrecker, there was no denying that. But a murderer?

Lana sucked up her breath, not wanting to broach the next subject, but needing answers. "Dotty, do you think Carl had much money or any possessions another could inherit?"

"What on earth are you talking about?"

"Jess said Carl had written up a will making her the beneficiary. And that he promised to leave her his yacht, *If the Shoe Fits*. But Sally said it's her boat."

"Oh Lord, what games was that boy playing? Carl always was the type to live beyond his means. No, Carl didn't own anything. Heck, I let him stay in one of my apartments for free whenever he was in Seattle. I sure hope he didn't promise it to Jessica. I don't want any trouble from that rabble-rouser when she gets back."

"I expect she'll give it a try. She's already threatening to hire a team of lawyers to sort this all out." Lana looked away, almost afraid to tell Dotty the rest. "There's more bad news. Carl also told Jess that he was the owner of Wanderlust Tours."

"He what?" Dotty screamed so loudly that Seymour jumped off the couch and sped out of the room. Rodney began to whimper as Chipper ducked under a chair.

Dotty bent down and patted her dogs' heads, reassuring them. "I'm sorry about scaring Seymour, but I cannot believe it. After all I did for that man! Even in death he's causing a heap of trouble." Dotty shook her head so violently, the entire screen shook.

"You listen to me, there is no way that Sally did this! You have to help my friend, at least until I can get her a lawyer," Dotty said, her tone furious, as she pointed a pudgy finger at Lana through the phone.

"I know you're upset, but I don't know how much I can really do for Sally. Her legal team will be able to do far more than I." Lana could see Dotty starting to protest. "But I promise I'll start looking into the guests' backgrounds and potential motives."

"Good. I'm going to call my lawyers and see what they can do. Tomorrow being New Year's Eve isn't going to speed the process up, but I reckon we'll have someone there to help Sally within twenty-four hours."

"Oh no, I completely forgot about New Year's Eve!"

"I know I'm asking a lot, but you're going to have to figure out a way to help Sally and give our guests a New Year's Eve to remember, Lana. They did pay a pretty penny for it, and I don't like giving refunds."

"Oh, man," Lana muttered. With everything going on, she'd forgotten that it was the end of the year. Dotty was right; making sure her guests enjoyed the New Year's celebrations was priority number one. Since they hardly knew Sally, Carl, or the Hendersons, their deaths and arrest weren't their concern.

"I'll do my best, starting with getting them to dinner on time. After I get them back to the hotel, I'll go online and see what I can find that might help Sally."

"You're a star, Lana. I really appreciate you helping me out."

"You're welcome. Give my Seymour a big kiss for me, will you?"

"You bet, hon."

24

Lana's To-Do List

As soon as Lana finished her call with Dotty, she rounded up the rest of her group and moved them to their final destination on the tour. Their hotel was situated in a gorgeous art deco building that Lana would have loved to explore. Unfortunately there was no time to do so. They were so late checking in, Lana had to ask her guests to reassemble in the lobby as soon as they'd freshened up, so that they wouldn't miss their dinner reservations.

When she ushered them into the taxi, Lana heard Helen say to Rebecca, "I would kill my husband if he treated me like that – cheating with another right under my nose. Did you know that Sally proposed to Carl, and not the other way around? Sally has been so unlucky in love, I bet she meant to kill him the first time she pushed him into the Danube. She must have finished off the job when he returned to the boat."

Lana couldn't hear Rebecca's response, but based on Helen's satisfied look, it was what Helen hoped to hear. Lana chose to tune her out. Sally's immediate future lay in her hands, and she had no idea who the real killer could be.

The dinner and folk dancing were a blur. Lana couldn't keep her mind on the performance or food; all she could think about was any possible connection between Carl and Margret Henderson.

After they were back in the hotel and all the guests' needs had been met, Lana changed into a pair of soft flannel pajamas and snuggled under the duvet. She balanced a notepad on her lap. Lana stared at the blank page, unsure where to start. It had been so long since she had investigated anyone.

In large loopy letters, she scribbled "TO-DO" at the top of the page. After a moment's hesitation, she wrote down a list of action items: "Investigate Tom's business and Helen's background. Jess – what's her story? Mrs. Margret Henderson – medical condition and connection to the others? Fabulous Five? Contact Jeremy."

Her old editor Jeremy should be able to help her with some of the details. Other than Christmas and birthday cards, they hadn't had much contact since they'd both been fired by the *Seattle Chronicle*. Yet she knew he still felt guilty that he had been able to find a new job straightaway, while she floundered to find her feet again in another profession. Maybe if she sent him a list of the passengers' names, he could look for dirt on any of them. Given the time of year, Lana hoped Jeremy was still checking his email somewhat regularly.

Before approaching Jeremy, Lana needed to search online first so as to not waste his time. She figured she'd get one shot at this, and then his feeling of guilt would be sated.

Once her laptop was warmed up, she started with the easiest. The Hendersons were exactly who Dotty said they were. Harold Henderson and Dotty's last husband had co-owned a seafood processing plant that had made them millionaires. Both Harold and Margret Henderson were active members of several charities. They had even founded one to help low-income families send their children to college. No wonder those two were so fit and with it – they were still incredibly active in their community.

Helen Roberts was the owner of Lake Union Yacht Rentals and had married Tom ten years earlier. After a bit more digging, Lana discovered that Helen had inherited the boat rental company and two more businesses from her father three years ago. Shortly after his father-in-law's death, Tom had been named the rental company's director. A few months ago, Helen had sold the other two businesses and invested the proceeds into the rental company, dramatically expanding their fleet of luxury yachts. Her name was also listed on several charities' boards, but none that the Hendersons were involved with. They also lived in different neighborhoods, and the Hendersons owned

116

no watercraft, as far as Lana could tell from the online information at her disposal. Lana made a note to ask Mr. Henderson about that, if she ever had the chance to speak with him again.

Tom Roberts's background was less auspicious. Before his marriage to Helen, he had founded several small companies in a range of fields, all of which had filed for bankruptcy years ago. *It is as if he has the kiss of death*, Lana thought. There was even a small article about his misfortune in the *Seattle Chronicle*, dated eleven years earlier. Yet three years ago, he was named the director of a multimillion-dollar boat rental company, one Helen's father had built up from scratch. Helen must have known that her husband was unsuccessful as a businessman. Had she made him the director simply for tax reasons? She was so domineering, Lana wouldn't be surprised if Helen was pulling the strings from behind the scenes. Though why she would hide her involvement was beyond Lana. Helen seemed obsessed with her social standing and making certain that everyone knew how rich she was.

Her fellow tour guide, Carl Miller, was an enigma. Lana found three references to him being arrested for insurance fraud and passing false checks, but all were several years old. Dotty had mentioned that Carl had been struggling with his gambling addiction for many years. He must have been stealing from and swindling people in order to fund his habit. From what she was reading, Carl had been a true con artist. Lana hoped Jeremy would be able to find out more about Carl's criminal background. It might provide them with clues as to who might want to hurt him. Lana knew she couldn't ask Dotty about it. That woman loved Carl like a son and was blind to his faults, as most mothers are. Lana hoped that Dotty would be able to accept whatever information she found out about Carl, even if it was bad.

Sally Simmons didn't exist, as far as social media and the internet were concerned. She had never been arrested, nor done anything noteworthy enough to have been reported on.

Other than her own social media, Lana found only one mention of Jess online. Her name was listed in the caption of a photo taken at her work during last year's Christmas party. Jess was standing on top of the bar, kissing its owner full on the lips. According to the caption, the woman standing off to the side with her hands on her hips, glaring at them, was his wife. The article's author even made a snotty reference to the threesome and the owner's sexual escapades. Somehow it seemed fitting. Jess was a true gold digger.

With reluctance, Lana typed in the names of the Fabulous Five, hoping they were innocent bystanders in this mess. She didn't know what she would do if she discovered Frieda or Sara were somehow connected to Carl. Soon she could put her mind at ease. Lana could find no connection between Carl and any of the five friends.

So where did that leave her? With a whole lot of questions and no real answers. She sure hoped her friend Jeremy could fill in some of the blanks.

25

A Visit from the Budapest Police

When the police inspector called her hotel room, Lana was half-asleep and groggy. His request to come downstairs to the lobby woke her right up. Lana threw on her clothes, hoping Sally was with him and being released.

Instead of Sally, Jess stood next to the inspector. They were deep in conversation. Based on Jess's defiant expression, she wasn't pleased.

Lana stood back and gave them room until Jess stormed off and ordered a daiquiri at the bar.

"Ah, Miss Hansen, thank you for seeing me at this late hour." He led them over to a corner of the lobby. "Please, have a seat. I have a few questions about Sally."

"Is she okay?"

"No, she is not, which is making it difficult for us to take her statement. Tell me, does Sally have reason to be depressed?"

"Yeah, you could say that. She had just found out that her fiancé had been messing around with Jess. I think it's safe to say her world fell apart."

"That would explain why she pushed Carl into the Danube."

"Yes, but she wasn't trying to kill him. It was a spur-of-the-moment decision, not premeditated," Lana insisted.

The detective gazed at her with narrowing eyes, yet said nothing.

"Why are you asking?" Lana pushed, hoping to find out when Sally would be released.

"She changed her statement about her pills. She says that she was going to kill herself by taking an overdose. She'd crushed them up and mixed them with water, but changed her mind and dumped them down the drain instead. Do you believe that this is plausible?"

Lana groaned internally. She should have never left Sally alone. "I guess it is possible. But what changed her mind?"

"She didn't want to give Carl the satisfaction."

"And you don't believe her?"

"No, that's the problem. I do believe her. She didn't want to make life easy for him by disappearing, but she couldn't stand to see him with Jess, either."

"And that's why you think she killed Carl and tried to kill Jess? That's ludicrous. My ex-husband cheated on me, and I didn't try to kill him."

"Perhaps if you'd had the opportunity…"

Lana glared at the inspector. "Are you going to keep Sally in custody or release her?"

"The autopsy results have led us to believe that Margret Henderson was poisoned. However, we won't know with what until we get the results from the toxicology screening back. Until we do, we will need to keep Sally in our custody."

"And how long will that take?"

"Four to six weeks."

"This is ridiculous! Sally didn't kill Carl or Mrs. Henderson. You aren't even searching for another suspect."

The detective smirked. "Of course we are. But until I know how Mrs. Henderson died, I cannot allow Sally Simmons to return to the United States."

Lana stood up, her arms trembling with rage. "I'm tired, and it's late. I look forward to seeing you again, when you release Sally."

The investigator stood up and left without another word.

26

A Liar and a Cheat

After the investigator left, Lana noticed Jess had gone outside to smoke a cigarette. Though Lana wanted to crawl back into bed, she wanted to talk to Jess even more. That curiosity led Lana out into the bitter cold.

Before she could say a word, Jess conceded, "Carl wasn't rich. He lied to me. The boat wasn't his, and neither was the tour company. I can't believe I trusted him." Jess mashed her cigarette out with her heel before lighting another.

Lana rubbed at her arms. "Did Carl really tell you that he owned them both?"

"Of course he did. Why do you think I followed him to Budapest?"

"Why did you? He'd already changed his will in your favor. What more did you want from him?"

"I thought if we spent two weeks together, I could persuade him to marry me."

"How did you get him to change his will, anyway?" Lana asked while rubbing at her cheeks.

"I told him it was over unless he made an honest woman out of me. He's the first one I'd landed who wasn't already married. This was my shot. He told me he just couldn't do it. He'd had too many ex-wives, and he knew how marriage changed things. So I kicked him out. Two days later he came crawling back with his will in his hands, showing me that he'd made me the primary beneficiary. He told me he'd rather I inherit everything, instead of his ex-wives."

Lana said, "Funny, he was never married."

Jess sighed and flicked her cigarette into the street. "It was all lies. If I had known that, I wouldn't have borrowed my mom's credit card to pay for this trip. She is going to kill me when I get home."

"You broke Sally's heart," Lana said through chattering teeth.

Jess leaned in so close that Lana could smell the nicotine on her breath. Her mouth twisted into a grimace. "She should thank me. I saved her a world of hurt. He would have sucked her dry and left her as soon as her bank account hit the single digits."

Lana pursed her lips and started to shake her head, but she knew Jess was right. Perhaps Carl's death was a blessing in disguise, at least as far as Sally was concerned. Assuming, of course, she wasn't convicted of causing it.

"Are you staying on for the rest of the trip?"

"I don't have much choice; I can't afford to fly back early. I might as well enjoy the rest of it." Jess turned on her heel and entered the lobby.

"Great," Lana muttered and trailed her inside.

27

Why Would I Leave Without a Fight?

Lana warmed her icy limbs by the lobby's fireplace before going back to her room. As she entered her hallway, Lana heard yelling and a lamp breaking. *Helen and Tom must be at it again,* she thought with a sigh. She hoped Dotty's travel insurance would cover those kinds of incidental expenses.

She put her ear to their door, only two away from her own, curious to see what this marital spat was about.

"Why would I leave without a fight?" Tom screamed.

"You've destroyed Dad's business. What more do you want?" Helen shot back, her voice vibrating with emotion.

"After putting up with your shenanigans for so long – everything," Tom retorted.

"You bastard! Your laziness ruined us. You don't deserve a penny."

Why do those two stay together? she mused. Lana shook her head, reminding herself that she was the last person in the world who should be judging other people's marriages. She sure hadn't seen the end of hers coming. Though based on their constant bickering, Lana hoped Tom and Helen would divorce soon, before one murdered the other.

Lana stood back from their hotel room door. She'd heard enough. As she opened her own, Lana thought back to the phone call Helen received in the riverboat's lounge. Why had Helen's accountant called her earlier? Helen said it was something to do with refinancing a mortgage. Perhaps the accountant had discovered something fishy about their finances that Tom hadn't yet told her about.

Lana added "Helen and Tom's finances?" to her to-do list. She would have to ask Jeremy about their financial situation as well as Carl's criminal background. Since she was awake, tonight was as good time as any to email Jeremy. Chances were great he was celebrating the holidays with relatives, but she had promised Dotty that she'd do everything she could to help Sally. And Dotty was the one person on this planet she did not want to disappoint. That woman had done so much for her, checking into her guests' backgrounds was the least she could do to repay her kindness.

28

Spa, Lunch, and Communist Statues

December 31 – Day Five of the Wanderlust Tour in Budapest, Hungary

Lana spent an hour typing up her questions for Jeremy before emailing them off. After finishing her cup of tepid tea, Lana fell into a deep sleep. Rippling water, fireworks, and banging doors filled her dreams. When she woke at 7:45 a.m., she didn't feel rested, even though she'd slept through her alarm.

Realizing she was supposed to be in the breakfast room greeting her guests in ten minutes, she pulled on the same clothes as yesterday and raced downstairs.

Luckily only the Fabulous Five were early. And from the looks of it, they were almost finished with breakfast.

"Ladies, how are you doing? Did everyone sleep well?"

"Never been better. I do like a good down comforter. And this one is a beauty. If it wasn't so bulky, I might try to sneak it home in my luggage." Sara giggled.

"Lana, why not grab some breakfast and join us?" Frieda asked, gesturing towards an empty chair.

"Don't mind if I do. Does anyone need anything else?"

After refreshing everyone's plates, Lana scooped up a bowl of yogurt and fresh fruit, then joined her guests.

"So, ladies, what tickles your fancy today? Memento Park, the city bus

125

tour, or Széchenyi Spa?" Lana asked, her tone innocent, as if she didn't know exactly what the Fabulous Five were planning on doing.

"The spa is calling our name. I want to get a full-body massage," Nicole said. "Have you been there yet, Lana? I hear the architecture is quite spectacular."

"You should join us," Frieda added.

"Oh, I guess I could," Lana said, realizing that she had nothing planned for her only free afternoon in the city. "The spa sounds great, actually. I need to make sure everyone gets on their buses and take care of some paperwork before I can leave. But I can come over and join you afterwards." She was flattered that they would invite her to tag along on their free day.

As Lana finished up her breakfast, Helen and Tom entered the room. Helen looked as if she hadn't slept a wink. Instead of her normal designer wear, she had on a faded pair of jeans and a loose-fitting T-shirt. Her eyes were puffy from crying, and the circles underneath were deep purple. In contrast, Tom was smartly dressed and chipper.

"Good morning, ladies," Tom called out to the Fabulous Five.

The ladies waved back tentatively, apparently as surprised by Tom's open attitude as Lana was.

Lana helped get them settled, then asked, "What is on your agenda today? Memento Park, the city bus tour, or Széchenyi Spa?"

"None of the above," Tom replied cheerfully. "I'm taking Helen to lunch at the New York Palace Café."

Lana's eyes widened in recognition. According to Dotty's guidebook, it was one of the most expensive restaurants in Budapest. "Oh, that's really generous of you."

"Nothing but the best for my wife, right darling?" Tom grabbed Helen's shoulder and pulled her close. Helen sighed deeply and looked away.

Just then, Jess appeared, sullen and withdrawn. She dished up her breakfast, then sat at an unoccupied table. The Fabulous Five's whispers kicked into overdrive.

"Hi, Jess. What would you like to do today?" Lana asked, doing her best to keep her tone light.

"I want to see the Communist statues."

"Great choice," Lana said, relieved Jess didn't want to visit the spa. That was one less drama to have to deal with today. Memento Park, an open-air museum filled with the Communist statues that once dotted the city, did sound intriguing. But right now, Lana was more interested in relaxing and taking in the spa's unique architecture than a history lesson. "The Memento Park trip does sounds like a fascinating tour. The bus will pick you up in an hour. Does that sound good?"

"Sure," Jess said, keeping her eyes on her food.

Lana headed to the reception desk to confirm her guests' reservations. After she'd sent Jess and the Fabulous Five off on their tours, Lana went upstairs to change her clothes and check for messages. Of course there were none; it was early morning on the West Coast, and Jeremy was probably still sleeping. Until he got in touch, there was nothing more she could do.

"I guess I'll have to go to the spa," she said, a smile splitting her face.

29

Széchenyi Spa

Lana couldn't believe the enormous orange and gray building before her was a spa. It looked more like a palace. After purchasing her ticket and finding the locker room, Lana slowly walked through the Széchenyi Baths Complex, taking in the impressive neo-baroque architecture and masses of happy bathers. There were eighteen pools and thermal baths her guests could be in. She started outside where, despite the falling snow, the pools were filled to the brim. The snowflakes melted in the steam hovering visibly above the warm water. Lana searched the faces of the many bathers, but didn't see the Fabulous Five. When she crisscrossed through the interior space, Lana was entranced by the marble columns and elegant railings marking off the many baths and swimming pools. It was so much more stylish than she could have imagined. Steam filled the rooms, making it more difficult to find her guests. After walking around in circles, Lana finally found Frieda, Rebecca, and Sara relaxing in one corner of a whirlpool.

"Lana, you made it! Climb on in. The temperature is perfect," Frieda said, moving over to make more room.

Lana sank slowly into the hot water. "This is the life," she said as she stretched out and leaned back. The gold details on the arches above seemed to glow in the steam-filled air.

After her body adjusted to the hot temperature, Lana asked, "Where are Nicole and Julia?"

"They're both getting massages. We wanted to unwind in the pools first," Sara explained.

All four women closed their eyes and sunk down into the water so that their chins rested on the surface. Bubbles from the jets tickled Lana's nose. Her short bob danced in the water. "This is the life, ladies," she murmured.

"So, Lana, did you always want to be a tour guide?"

"No, it was a last-minute decision," Lana said, her tone guarded. She didn't know how the ladies would react if they knew this was her first tour.

"Oh, what did you do before?" Rebecca asked.

"I was an investigative journalist for eleven years, before I lost my job."

"Oh, the recession destroyed the job market, didn't it?"

Lana sighed heavily. She couldn't lie to them. "It wasn't that I couldn't find work. No newspaper would touch me with a ten-foot pole."

"I don't understand," Frieda said.

"I discovered a wood-processing plant was releasing contaminants into local waterways, causing massive salmon deaths. My source had documents showing how the company was bribing the inspectors. Their lawyer cried libel and sued my newspaper. Unfortunately my source refused to go on record after his family was threatened, meaning we lost the case and my editor and I lost our jobs."

"Oof. That's got to sting," Rebecca said.

"You could say that. Since then, I've worked as a tour guide and yoga instructor."

"At least you have your health," Frieda added, patting her arm.

"Just because you can't write for newspapers doesn't mean you can't write anymore. Heck, there are tons of writers making money with their blogs and as freelance writers. Never give up," Sara said firmly.

Lana chuckled. "I appreciate your enthusiasm, but simply having my name in the byline would trigger a lot of hate mail."

"You could always use a pen name," Sara pushed.

Lana frowned. "I don't know."

"Never say never, as the saying goes," Sara said.

Lana ducked her head under the water, not wanting to continue the conversation. When she broke through the surface, Lana stared up at the ceiling, considering Sara's words. Why couldn't she write again? Not for profit, but to feed her soul. Writing had always been the one thing she was good at, and not doing it was like living with one arm tied behind her back. After the libel lawsuit and the backlash she'd had from every other newspaper she contacted, she hadn't dared write anything again. Freelance work was out of the question. Yet Lana had never considered blogging for fun.

She would have to use a pen name. The last thing she wanted was to be trolled online by the wood-processing plant employees or any of her former colleagues – many of whom didn't believe that she'd truly had a source. Lana knew their hurtful whispers were born from their jealousy. But looking back, she wished that someone else had gotten the scoop and that she'd never written that damn story.

"So what does your reporter's nose tell you?" Rebecca said, interrupting Lana's thoughts. "Did Sally really do it? I can hardly believe that she is capable of killing anyone, but it's not looking good for her," Rebecca said, blunt as ever.

"I cannot believe she would hurt Carl, as much as she may have wanted to. She loved that man to bits," Sara said.

"Okay, if Sally didn't do it, who did? Who is the killer in our group?" Frieda asked, a mischievous twinkle in her eye.

"Agatha Christie said that most murders were committed for one of four reasons: jealousy, greed, a desire for power, and revenge," Sara responded.

"I didn't know you read her mysteries!" Frieda exclaimed.

"Of course I do. She and E.L. James are my favorite authors; I've read all of their novels."

"Do you mean the woman who wrote *Fifty Shades of Grey*?" Lana sputtered.

"That trilogy really gets my heart racing," Sara tittered.

"Then they'd be against my doctor's orders. My blood pressure's already too high, and reading those books might mess with my medications," Rebecca snickered.

"Can I borrow one from you after we get home?" Frieda asked.

"When do you have time to read, Frieda? You're obsessed with soap operas,"

Sara said, disdain in her voice.

"I've been watching *General Hospital* for thirty years now. It's an addiction, I admit it. If only they'd end the darn show, then I'd have more time to read."

"Or you could turn the television off," Sara offered.

"Once you start, you can't stop. They're like potato chips," Frieda said.

"Or cocaine," Rebecca added, nodding knowingly.

Frieda slapped the water, sending bubbles flying. "Ladies, who is the murderer?"

"If it makes you feel better, I don't think it's one of you. Nor do I think the Hendersons had anything to do with it. None of you knew Carl, nor did you have reason to harm him," Lana said.

"Well, that's a relief," Rebecca said.

"So that leaves Jess, Helen, and Tom," Sara said.

"You can't forget Sally. She did have a good reason for wanting Carl dead."

"You do have a point, Frieda. Let us consider her motive first," Rebecca said.

"Sally pushed Carl into the Danube," Frieda said.

"In a fit of rage," Lana interjected.

"What if she realized how easy it was to push him in and decided to try again when everyone was sleeping?" Rebecca suggested. "The way he was carrying on was shameful. I would have wanted to kill my husband if he'd done that to me."

"I don't know. Do you really believe Sally killed Carl or tried to kill Jess? She just doesn't seem like the type," Lana said.

"It's the nice ones that snap when they finally crack," Frieda said.

"She does have the strongest motive, Lana," Sara added. "And she can't explain where the missing pills went. If Mrs. Henderson was poisoned, it might have been with Sally's medication."

Lana considered telling the ladies about Sally's suicide attempt, but rejected the idea. It was too personal to share. "Does anyone really think she meant to kill Mrs. Henderson?"

"She was probably trying to kill Jess. They were sitting at the same table."

"But how? She couldn't have crushed up the pills and put them in the carafes of tea and coffee before you all returned from Visegrád! I was there the whole – oh…" Lana's voice trailed off.

"What do you remember?"

"Sally helped me set out the cups and carafes before you all returned. I guess I did leave her alone in the lounge when I went down to the pier to greet you."

"So she had the motive and opportunity," Rebecca confirmed.

"But there were no assigned seats. She couldn't have chosen the placement of the guests. And there is no way Jess would have listened to her if Sally had tried. How could she have known where anyone would be sitting?"

"For all you know, she guided Mrs. Henderson to that chair, knowing Jess would sit with them instead of us."

"But if she did poison a carafe of tea, everyone who drank from it should have gotten sick or at least drowsy. Right?"

"Maybe she poured Jess a cup and dumped it out before anyone else could drink from it."

"I don't know, I think I would have noticed," Lana said.

"Poor Margret. I guess the police will soon know whether she died of natural causes or not," Sara said, shaking her head.

"I don't know how Sally did it, but even you have to admit that her case isn't looking good, Lana," Frieda said.

"Before you all convict Sally, shall we consider the rest, starting with Jess?" Lana asked.

"Why would Jess kill Carl?" Rebecca asked.

"If he married Sally, she would miss out on the inheritance. But as it stands, she's the beneficiary."

"But there is no inheritance," Sara protested.

"Jess didn't know that until after he died. If she truly believed that Carl had left her a yacht and successful business, then she must have been terrified to find out Carl was going to marry another. Surely he would change his will to benefit Sally if they did. That could explain why she'd killed him in a fit of passion," Lana pushed. Though she wasn't convinced Jess did it, the young waitress was still at the top of her suspect list. Lana scolded herself for not paying more attention to her guests' comings and goings the night Carl died.

"Jess might be a marriage-breaking hussy, but I don't believe she's the murdering kind. Finding another sucker to sponge off of sure seems easier than murder," Frieda said dismissively.

"Okay, what about Helen and Tom?"

"What about them? Those two socialites didn't know Carl, did they?" Frieda asked.

"I did hear Carl and Tom fighting when we were in the labyrinth. Tom demanded that Carl return money he'd given him, but Carl had gambled it all away. So they must have met before coming on this tour."

"Were they business partners?"

"I don't know," Lana admitted.

"You can't get blood from a stone. Maybe when Tom realized Carl would never pay him back, he got mad and accidentally killed him?" Frieda offered.

"Frieda, you have an excellent point," Lana said. Since Carl's death, Tom had seemed far more assured of himself, even daring to stand up to his wife. *He must be so relaxed because he thinks he got away with murder*, Lana thought. "The brandy!"

"Do you want a shot of brandy now? It's too early for me. That stuff set fire to my throat."

"No, the bottles of fruit brandy Tom bought in Visegrád. I thought it was strange that he offered to share shots with the group. And Helen carries Valium in her purse. He must have been worried that Jess would tell Helen about his deal with Carl, so he tried to poison her with his wife's drugs."

"Jess did insinuate that she'd overheard Tom and Carl reviewing business contracts while waitressing," Frieda confirmed.

"Oh no, is Helen in danger?" Sara asked.

"I don't think so," Lana said. "If Tom really did push Carl overboard and try to poison Jess, he did it to prevent Helen from discovering his secret. If he was going to kill her, you would think he would have just poisoned Helen, instead of going to the trouble of killing the others."

"True, though I still think we should tell her," Sara said.

"But how could we, without Tom finding out that we suspect him?" Lana asked.

"And what about Jess?" Sara pressed. "We can't just let him try again, can we?"

"No, I suppose not," Lana grumbled, not relishing the thought of keeping Jess close. "We'll have to let her know about Tom, or at least what we suspect."

"If Tom really is a murderer, then he must be pretty pleased that Sally has been taken into custody," Rebecca said.

"If he thinks he got away with it, he might let his guard down and slip up," Lana said. "Until we have solid proof, all we can do is watch him."

30

Jeremy Gets in Touch

When it was 7 a.m. in Seattle, Lana left the ladies in the Finnish sauna and headed back to the hotel. A quick check of her email revealed a new message from Jeremy, sent minutes earlier. *Thank God for early risers*, she thought then dialed his number, eager to know what he'd discovered.

"Hey, Jeremy. Any luck reaching your contacts?"

"Of course not, it's the holidays. Most people are with their families."

Lana sighed. "I figured it would be too easy if you had."

"But you are in luck. However, before I share this information with you, you have to promise not to tell anyone about it. It is part of an exclusive story we are going to publish on January 3."

"I don't exactly move in the same circles as I used to. Your secret is safe with me."

"My news editor is writing an exposé about a Ponzi scheme and the suckers they lured in. Forty local business owners invested in a new plastic recycling plant that would have been built on Bainbridge Island. They transferred millions into a fund earmarked for its construction. The only problem is, the investment management firm never intended to build the plant. Once they hit their goal, they flew the coop. The money is gone. It looks like Tom was one of the investors. He'd pumped almost two hundred thousand dollars into the fund over the past six months."

"The kiss of death strikes again," Lana mumbled. Tom had absolutely no business sense.

"As part of her story, my news editor did some digging into Tom's background and discovered that his yacht rental company got hit badly during a recent storm. And it looks like they were underinsured. With such a large fleet, it will cost a fortune to get them all up and running again."

"Tom is really in over his head, isn't he?" Lana said. His fleet of rental yachts was busted, and he lost two hundred thousand in bad investments. What a sucker. How could Helen stay with him?

"There is one more thing, but my Lifestyle editor wasn't certain if it was a mistake or not."

"Go on."

"Helen's lawyer filed for divorce two days ago. Last night, she annulled the documents."

"What do you mean?"

"I mean her lawyer withdrew the divorce petition, meaning Helen is no longer seeking to part from her husband. Though it does look like she was intending to do so only two days ago. And she had a prenuptial agreement, so Tom wouldn't have gotten a penny. Like I said, my editor isn't certain if there was a mix-up with either the filing or withdrawal. It happened so fast, it almost seems like a glitch. But a juicy one I thought you would be interested in."

"Jeremy, none of this makes much sense right now, but I'm certain it will soon. You've been a big help, my friend."

"I'm sorry I couldn't do more for you. I can ask my contacts about your other questions after New Year's Day."

"There's no need. Sally should have a lawyer by the end of the day, and they'll take over the investigation. Thanks, Jeremy. And happy New Year."

"You too, Lana."

Lana stared at the receiver, processing the information Jeremy had just passed along. She wasn't surprised that Helen had filed for divorce; she and Tom fought like cats and dogs. But the timing was so strange. Here they were on vacation, while her lawyer was starting a legal chain of events that would end their marriage. Then, before it could even get going, he stopped the process. So where did that leave Helen and Tom? *Still married, I guess*, Lana thought, *though not happily.* What had happened last night to make Helen change her mind?

31

Power and Revenge

Lana readjusted her pantyhose and took a long look in the hotel room mirror. As she twirled around in her flapper-style dress, she couldn't help but smile. She looked good for thirty-seven. Since her divorce had become final, she had rarely gone out. The idea of seeing couples in love had kept her home. If anything, this trip to Budapest had reminded her that there was still a world waiting to be explored. After she got back to Seattle, she'd have to go out more. Who knew? She might yet find her prince on a white horse.

When she went down to the lobby to meet her group, they were all enjoying cocktails while waiting for the bus to arrive.

Tom was regaling the group with his latest business idea – riverboat cruises from Seattle to Vancouver Island. "I've already been in touch with a local shipbuilder. He thinks he could get me ten straightaway and another five or so by March."

Lana's eyebrows rose automatically.

"They aren't meant to sail on the ocean, Tom. That's why they are called riverboats," Helen chastised. Tom ignored her, instead continuing on about his plan as if she hadn't spoken.

Riverboats? Lana thought. Helen must be livid. Tom had already ruined her yacht rental business. There was no way someone like Helen would stay with someone like Tom willingly. *What is he holding over her?* Lana wondered. They continued to bicker, making most of the other guests visibly uncomfortable. Lana was afraid things were going to come to a head when Helen suddenly stood up and ran into the lobby's bathroom.

Tom called out, "'Til death do us part," as Helen stormed off. When the bus arrived minutes later, Lana wasn't certain Helen would join them. But Tom went to fetch his wife, and whatever he said to her brought her out of the bathroom and into the van without another word.

The moonless night and falling snow made it feel as if they were driving through a tunnel. When they arrived at the Hungarian State Opera House, the first thing Lana noticed was the dramatic lighting. The opera house was only three stories tall, but each level was grandly decorated with delicate porticos and statues. The arched entryway loomed high above the visitors congregating around the entrance. Lana's jaw dropped when they walked into the foyer. The ceiling was richly decorated with frescos and gold molding. The grand staircase, made of white stone and marble, seemed to snake through the expansive lobby. Lana was afraid to step on the red carpet for fear of dirtying it. The highly polished walls reflected the lights and sounds of happy patrons. Everything sparkled and shone. It was incredible.

"Where are we sitting?" Rebecca asked, breaking the spell.

"Let me get our tickets." Lana looked around until she spotted the box office. Dotty said their tickets would be waiting there for them. When Lana approached, she noticed they rented opera glasses. "Does anyone want to use these?" She pointed at the sign.

"No thanks. I'd rather watch the show and not worry about trying to follow the singers around," Frieda explained.

"Good point, Frieda. Anyone else?"

"We have our own pair," Helen said.

"Okay, let me rent one for myself, then we'll find our seats."

Lana searched for the correct entrance, then led her group into the main auditorium.

"Holy cow," Lana whispered, completely taken aback by the beauty of it all. A massive chandelier hung in the center of the dome-like ceiling. Elegant frescoes of angels playing musical instruments circled the lighting fixture. Three levels of seating were built into the sides of the horseshoe-shaped auditorium; the yellow stone glowed against the red walls, floors, and seats. The tourist guidebooks weren't lying when they said this opera house was one of the most beautiful in the world.

A uniformed attendant handed them all brochures summarizing the opera's plot, then led them to their seats. Her group was sitting three rows behind the orchestra pit. Lana felt like a princess. She only hoped her dress was formal enough. Lana was anxiously comparing her clothes to the other patrons' dresses, when Helen said, "Oh, they have boxes here. I wonder if one is still available."

Before Lana could react, Helen was already walking back to the box office with Tom in tow. Lana tagged along, curious to see whether Helen would be successful.

When Helen inquired, the ticket seller's face lit up. "We do have a last-minute cancellation. It is a box on the third tier, on the far left."

"Excellent, I'll take it." Helen lay her ticket down on the counter to get her credit card out. The seller noticed her current seating placement. "Your seats on the floor do have better views of the stage than this box. Are you certain you wish to switch places?"

"Oh yes, I am quite certain."

The ticket seller shrugged and charged her credit card.

When Lana saw the price, she almost choked. How could Helen afford the tickets? Did she even know that she was broke? As tempting as it was to say something, Lana bit her tongue. It wasn't her place, and she didn't yet know all the facts.

Tom kissed her cheek. "We deserve only the best, right, Helen?"

Helen's smile made Lana's skin crawl. Tom took her arm as they ascended the grand staircase to their private box. *So much for keeping an eye on him,* Lana thought.

When Lana returned to her group, Frieda stood up and announced, "I want to sit on the end, in case I have to use the toilet. We saved you this seat." Frieda pointed to the one next to her. Lana squeezed in next to Sara, sinking deep into the comfortable chair. They were perfectly situated to see both into the orchestra pit and the entire stage.

Lana dutifully opened the brochure and skimmed the brief summary of the opera.

Sara leaned over Lana to read the pamphlet to Frieda. "It's a one-act opera by Richard Strauss. Oh no, it's a hundred minutes long, with no intermission."

"Great, I hope my bladder can make it through," Frieda grumbled.

"*Elektra* is a story of power and revenge. Her mother kills her father, and Elektra vows vengeance," Sara explained.

"Geez, what kind of play is this? Couldn't they have picked something lighter for New Year's Eve?" Frieda grumbled.

"This is the most frequently performed opera in the world, at least of those based on classic Greek mythology," Lana said, repeating what she'd just read.

"Great, philosophy was always my weakest subject," Sara said.

"Mythology," Lana corrected.

"Oh, I always thought that the Greeks invented mythology as a way of illustrating their philosophy."

Lana pondered her statement for a moment. "I never thought of it that way before."

Moments later, the lights dimmed until only the exits were illuminated. Lana looked to her companions and smiled.

Trumpets blared as the curtains lifted, startling them all. Filling the stage was an off-kilter wall with large openings spaced sporadically over its surface. It was gray and devoid of decoration, reminding Lana of a Soviet-era apartment building lying on its side. Red and blue spotlights lit up the openings, casting the singers standing inside of each in a creepy light. At center stage stood a woman in a dirty robe, her hair a bird's nest, her face covered with black streaks.

Above the stage, the subtitles lit up, translating the text. "You should not take pleasure in my pain..." sang the lead character while gesturing dramatically towards her mother. The singer's demeanor and delivery were electrifying. Her voice was impassioned with a soul-crushing sadness.

Whoever this Elektra was, she was wild, crazy, and obviously going mad, Lana thought. It was an intense, violent world, and the music fit perfectly. The musical score was much more modern than Lana had expected. It was at times bombastic and chaotic, and moments later melodious and soothing. The action on stage reminded Lana of Helen and Tom's relationship. She frequently looked up towards their private box, but it was so dark that she could not see them.

A few minutes into the opera, Frieda leaned over to Sara and whispered, "Why do they keep screaming at each other? I can't understand a single word."

"I think they're singing in German," Sara whispered back. "Why don't you read the subtitles?"

"My glasses are for reading, but not at that long a distance."

"Shh," said the woman sitting behind Frieda. She glared at Lana for good measure.

"Why don't you switch places with me?" Lana whispered into Sara's ear.

"I'm fine where I'm at," Sara said while jutting her chin.

Lana ignored the woman behind them and focused on what was happening on stage. Soon she was swept up in the tragic story. This was her first real opera, and Lana was blown away by the magnitude. It was so much more than just the music. The costumes, scenery, lighting, props, and emotionally charged acting made it a powerful and compelling performance. *If only the topic was less depressing*, she thought. A story of murder and revenge was indeed a strange way to ring in the new year.

When the onstage lighting brightened to illuminate the front of the podium, Lana realized she could now see Tom and Helen quite clearly through her rented opera glasses. To her surprise, they were chatting animatedly while gesturing towards the stage. Looking at them now, no one would suspect that they'd barely spoken to each other during the past few days. *What changed to make Helen come out of her shell?* Lana wondered. Tom stood and leaned over the railing while looking through their opera glasses. *Their view must not be that great, just like the ticket seller told them*, Lana realized.

"I don't understand. Why did the mother murder the father and son?" Frieda asked.

"Shh," said the woman behind them, this time leaning in close to Lana's ear as she hushed them.

"Okay, back off lady," Lana growled. The older woman pulled back.

"Power and prestige," Sara whispered.

"Would you kill your own son and husband for that? She must have known her daughters would try to avenge their father's death," Frieda mused.

"That's why she tried to lock them up in an insane asylum," Sara said.

"Greek tragedies are really twisted."

"Greek tragedies are based on human behavior. In this case, greed. Those with power or social standing are often so afraid of losing it that they flaunt it, out of insecurity. You only have to look at people like Helen and Tom to believe it. And when they are threatened with losing their perceived power, they can strike out at the most unexpected moments," Sara said.

"What do you mean, Helen and Tom?" Lana asked. She glanced up at their box and saw Helen was taking her turn with the theater binoculars. Helen leaned so far over the railing that Lana was afraid she was going to fall over. Helen began pointing at something on the far right of the stage. Lana looked but couldn't see what she found so fascinating. Was there a singer offstage that Helen could see from up there? Tom stood up next to his wife to better see what interested her. Helen handed him the opera glasses.

"I wouldn't be surprised if Helen and Tom were broke, mortgaged to the hilt and living far beyond their means. Those types usually are," Frieda said.

"As if you would know," Sara hissed.

"My husband was an insurance adjuster. I would know," Frieda shot back. "I still don't understand why Elektra wants to kill her mother instead of having her brought to trial. Wouldn't that be true justice?"

"Would you please be quiet!" the woman behind them whispered.

"If this Strauss guy had built in an intermission, I could have read the brochure and would know what this was about, instead of having to ask," Frieda grumbled.

In the hope of staving off a fight, Lana squinted in the low light to read the rest to Frieda. "Elektra thinks killing her mother is the only way she will be able to put an end to her maddening dreams and find the peace she seeks. Only after her mother is dead will she be able to let go of the hatred she's held on to for so long. But her bloodlust for vengeance ultimately destroys her."

"Tragic," Frieda murmured.

"That is enough!" the woman behind them said in a normal tone of voice. However, in this opera house with its perfect acoustics, it sounded as if she was shouting. Several rows turned to look for the source. Even the singers on stage seemed momentarily jarred by the outburst.

Lana shrunk down into her chair, wishing she could disappear, before remembering that she was the guide and thus responsible for her guests.

Lana turned to the woman behind them. "I am so sorry. It won't happen again."

Frieda leaned close to Lana and murmured in her ear, "I bet she and Helen would get along fabulously. She's one of those uppity types, as well. Did you see her scarf? That's hand-painted silk. I bet it cost a fortune. But her dress has been altered too many times. Did you see the fraying at the sleeves? With those types, it's all about keeping up appearances," Frieda said, her tone smug.

Suddenly Lana felt as if she was falling down a dark tunnel. *Oh no, could it be that simple?*

Snippets of information raced through Lana's head: refinanced mortgages, discounted vacations, and a business about to go bankrupt. And then there were the damaged yachts and Tom's Ponzi scheme investments.

Tom had ruined her. Helen filing for divorce made perfect sense. Her social standing might be tarnished by divorcing him, but it would be easy enough for her to convince her friends that Tom was the bad guy in their relationship. Heck, they'd probably cheer her for getting rid of him.

So why did Helen annul the divorce proceedings? Tom must be holding something over her head to have made her stay.

Helen was livid with Carl, so much so that she followed him to the casino and threatened him. Could she have confronted him on the riverboat and killed him when he refused to return their money? Yes, Lana could easily imagine that she could have.

So how did Mrs. Henderson fit into all of this? Was she the target, or was it Jess? Mrs. Henderson was almost invisible on this trip. She seemed happy to go along for the ride and certainly didn't upset anyone. Except for the night Carl died and she couldn't sleep because of all the noises. *Oh no*, Lana moaned. The doors opening and closing kept Mrs. Henderson awake. And she blamed "that girl" for keeping her up.

What if the girl Mrs. Henderson was referring to was Helen and not Jess? Mrs. Henderson died shortly after Lana told her group that the police were going to question them about the night Carl disappeared. If Mrs. Henderson told them that she'd seen Helen in the hallway, her statement would contradict Helen's alibi.

What if Helen did push Carl into the Danube and Tom figured it out? He could be using that as blackmail to stay married. Tom's life had improved dramatically since Carl's death, but not Helen's. At the beginning of the trip, Helen dominated their relationship. That all changed after Carl's body was found.

Yet someone like Helen wouldn't be able to demurely sit by and watch Tom destroy her father's business. What if she thought the only way to free herself from Tom was to kill him – just like Elektra?

Lana looked up to their box. Tom was leaning far over the railing, gazing through the opera glasses. Helen's arms were coiling back like a snake ready to strike. Lana jumped out of her chair. "It's Helen! She killed Carl and Mrs. Henderson!"

"That is enough. Security!" the woman behind Lana shrieked so loudly that she momentarily drowned out the opera.

Tom startled at the noise and leaned back into the box as he looked down, exactly at the same moment that Helen's hand shot out to push him. Her arms slid over his back, yet the momentum was enough to force him over the balustrade. As Tom fell headfirst, he grabbed onto a rail and hung on for dear life.

"Helen is trying to kill her husband! Someone help him – there, in the box!" Lana screamed as she pointed up. A spotlight whipped around until it found Tom. Helen was clawing at his hand, trying to loosen his grip. When the light hit her, she sprung up like a cat and ran out of the box.

Moments later, other patrons raced to Tom's rescue, earning a loud round of applause as they pulled him up to safety.

32

What Was The Catch?

Once again, the police took statements from Lana and her group, this time in the lobby of the opera house, after which they were allowed to return to their seats. Lana shared all of the information she had discovered about her guests, persuading the police that this was not an accident, but a murder attempt.

After she'd been released, Lana excused herself from the group and found a quiet place to talk. She thought it prudent to call Dotty before the Budapest police contacted her.

Luckily it was early afternoon in Seattle. Dotty answered on the fifth ring. It took Lana a few minutes to get her up to speed.

"I don't understand why Helen wouldn't just divorce Tom. Why did she try to kill him?"

"Tom must have been embezzling from her boat rental company in order to invest in that plastic recycling plant. Unfortunately for him, it was a Ponzi scheme, and he lost everything he invested. Helen mentioned that her home was double-mortgaged. It doesn't sound like they had a lot of cash on hand. When the rental fleet was damaged in that storm, I bet there wasn't enough money left to fix them all. Especially considering his company was underinsured. Helen filed for divorce right after her accountant called, then withdrew her petition two days later. I bet Tom figured out that she killed Carl and was holding it over her. If Helen divorced him, he would have nothing. But he had destroyed her father's legacy. I can imagine the thought of being stuck with Tom drove her to murder."

"How the heck does Carl fit into this?" Dotty asked. Lana wasn't sure whether it was the static on the line or the sadness in her heart, but Dotty sounded terrible.

"Jess saw them reviewing maintenance contracts at the café where she works. I think Carl had somehow convinced Tom that he could get his yachts fixed for less than the going rate."

"What was the catch?"

"Apparently Tom discovered that Carl was lying and demanded his money back. But it was too late. Carl had already gambled it away. That's what I overheard in the labyrinth."

"So Tom killed Carl?"

"No, Helen did. She confronted Carl at the casino but got kicked out by security. I think she waited on the upper deck and confronted him about the money. I wouldn't be surprised if he laughed at her like he did Tom. Helen does have quite a temper. I bet she didn't mean to kill him."

"But she did. Carl is dead. Oh, poor Sally. What a nightmare. But why did Margret Henderson have to die?"

"I don't know for certain. I suspect it is because Mrs. Henderson's statement about the night Carl died would have contradicted Helen's. Tom admitted to poisoning Mrs. Henderson, so she was the intended victim, not Jess. The police have both Tom and Helen in custody."

"Good. If Tom had anything to do with either of the deaths, he should pay for it, as well."

Chimes rang through the lobby, signaling that the opera was about to resume. Dotty must have heard it, too.

"Lana, take good care of my group, or what's left of them anyway. I sure hope you enjoy the New Year's celebrations tonight. I'll see you tomorrow."

Lana's eyes widened when she looked at her watch. In two hours, this year would be over. She could not wait to start anew. "Happy New Year, Dotty!"

33

Happy New Year!

After the police were finished questioning several patrons, the opera resumed as if nothing had happened. The final curtain was drawn to a tremendous applause.

Lana, still in a daze, escorted her group back to the Danube for their final celebration. Dotty had originally booked a champagne cruise at midnight, but Lana thought it was too soon for any of them to board another boat. Yesterday, with the hotel receptionist's help, Lana had arranged for her group to celebrate New Year's Eve at a fancy restaurant with a terrace overlooking Chain Bridge.

At ten to midnight, her group reassembled outside, champagne in hand, as they waited for the world-famous fireworks show to commence. When Lana stepped out onto the balcony, the cold wind whipped through her clothes, and wisps of snow settled on her hair. But the views made her stay. Chain Bridge was so close, she felt as if she could touch it. The thousands of lights illuminating the many bridges and monuments were reflected in the waters of the Danube, turning the river into fluid diamonds.

Loud speakers counted down the minutes. When they reached the last seconds of the year, her group joined in, all screaming at the top of their lungs. Lana felt pure bliss bubbling to the surface. In a few seconds, this year would be over, and a new one would begin. A new year full of new possibilities. Lana could not wait.

The massive crowds lining both sides of the river yelled out in unison, "Three, two, one!"

Fireworks exploded across the Danube, lighting up the cityscape with gigantic balls of color. The deep explosions drowned out any conversation. Lana's group stood side by side at the railing, stunned by the beauty of this perfect night. Despite all of the drama, Lana had really enjoyed leading this group. Considering the high body count, she doubted Dotty would hire her again. But it was a new career option to consider. Lana pushed thoughts of the future out of her mind and let herself get caught up in the festive spirit of renewal.

As the last burst lit up the night, it seemed as if all of Budapest erupted in applause. Lana's heart burst with joy. The worst year of her life was now officially over. Tears of happiness trickled down her frozen cheeks.

"Happy New Year!" she screamed, kissing and hugging her tour group as if they were close friends. Best of all, her guests hugged her back with all their might.

It was going to be a great year.

34

Last Breakfast in Budapest

January 1 – Day Six of the Wanderlust Tour in Budapest, Hungary

The new year began with a headache for Lana Hansen. A pounding sensation in her brain woke her early and had her guzzling water in the bathroom until she felt human again. Lana wasn't much of a drinker, but last night her entire tour group had overindulged, and she'd joined in willingly.

Lana crawled back into bed and slept more soundly than she had in months. When a distant beeping broke through her scattered dreams, she used one finger to lift her eyelid and find the source. Her alarm clock was beckoning her.

"Nuts, breakfast time," she mumbled.

It was their last day in Budapest, and her job this morning was to rush her group through breakfast and get them into an airport shuttle bus by eleven. It was already seven-thirty, and she hadn't yet packed up her bags. Lana shot out of bed, threw open her suitcase, and tossed all of her clothes inside. They didn't fit as well as when they were neatly folded, but it would have to do. Most would need to be washed as soon as she returned home, anyway.

As soon as her bags were ready to go, Lana skipped down to the breakfast room, curious to see who was already present. Not surprisingly, the Fabulous Five were tucking into breakfast. The extra person at their table brought a smile to Lana's face.

"Sally, you're back!" Lana wrapped her up in a hug. Sally held her tight, wiping away a tear when they pulled apart. "What happened? Did the police release you?"

"Yes, they did. Whatever Helen and Tom told them, they are finally convinced that I didn't kill Carl or Margret Henderson."

The police inspector who had arrested Sally entered the breakfast room. He was finishing up a call in Hungarian. As soon as he hung up, he came over to Lana and gave her his hand.

"Good morning, do you have a moment to talk?"

"Of course," Lana said, surprised by his polite tone. His eyes were bloodshot, and there was a thick layer of black stubble on his chin. Lana wondered whether he had slept at all since she saw him last. She led them to the lobby, well away from the Fabulous Five's prying ears.

"I thought you should know that we have completed our questioning of Helen and Tom Roberts. They are responsible for both murders."

"Was I right about Helen's motives? Was it purely for financial reasons?"

The inspector shrugged. "Helen maintains that when Carl returned from the casino, he tried to force himself on her. While running away from him, she hit him with the rescue hook, and he went overboard. She claims she didn't tell her husband because she was ashamed."

"Do you believe her?"

"Not really. We found video footage of her fighting with Carl in the casino. Your friends were right; she was demanding that Carl return several thousand dollars that he'd taken from her husband. We are in contact with the Seattle police, though I doubt we will ever know what really happened that night on the boat."

"And Tom? Did he kill Mrs. Henderson?" Lana still couldn't call her Margret.

"Tom and Helen worked together on that one. Helen was worried Margret Henderson would tell us about seeing her in the hallway late at night, thus contradicting her alibi. She crushed up several of her Valium pills, and Tom added them to a shot of *pálinka* that Mrs. Henderson drank after they'd returned from Visegrád."

"Helen told you that?"

"No, Tom did. He is cooperating fully. Frankly, I think he's scared of what his wife might do to him if she's set free."

Lana puffed out her cheeks. "It is such a relief knowing that neither will get away with these murders. Thank you. I'll inform the owner of Wanderlust Tours about your findings."

When Lana returned to the breakfast room, Jess had joined the Fabulous Five. She was sitting next to Nicole and directly across from Sally. Lana's steps slowed as she worried about the impending confrontation, but it seemed as if Jess and Sally had called a truce. Lana glanced at the empty chairs, her thoughts turning to Carl and Margret.

Both Jess and Sally were probably better off without Carl. The man was a con artist incapable of love. But poor Mr. Henderson; his wife died for nothing.

She felt a tear coming on until she recalled his words about life and love. At least they'd had sixty-seven wonderful years together. Ron's betrayal had broken her spirit and trust in men. But there were plenty more fish in the sea, as Dotty would say. She was only thirty-seven; there was more than enough time to fall in love again.

Too soon, it was time to go to the airport. Their departure was a flurry of embraces and tears. Sara made a point of pulling Lana aside so they could talk more easily. "You are a wonderful guide; all of us girls think so. I'll be sure to tell Dotty how much you helped us enjoy Budapest, despite all of the problems."

Lana gently squeezed her shoulder. "Thank you, Sara. But I doubt Dotty will ask me to work for her again."

Sara cocked her head and raised an eyebrow.

"The two bodies?"

Sara waved her words away. "That can happen to anyone. You didn't kill Carl or Margret. It's not your fault someone else did. I'm sure it'll all work out."

"Thanks, Sara." Lana smiled at the older lady, not believing a word she said. She began to pick up her bag when a sudden thought made her stop and address the group. "Oh, could I ask you all for one last favor…"

Minutes later, the airport announcement system crackled to life. Their plane was boarding. They waved at each other from their seats, scattered around the airplane, until the door closed and the stewardesses asked them to buckle up. Lana took her place by the window. As much as she wanted to stretch out, she couldn't bring herself to use Carl's reserved seat, empty beside her.

35

Snuggling with Seymour

January 2 – Seattle, Washington

"You're right. The fresh ginger is zesty," Dotty said. Her curlers were out, and the resulting ringlets hugged her heart-shaped face. She and Lana sat in Dotty's living room, sipping tea while Lana recounted her adventures in Budapest. Rodney was in Dotty's lap, his curled tail twitching as she scratched at his back. Chipper chewed on a fake bone, his tail thumping against the couch in rhythm with his bites.

Seymour was spread across Lana's lap, purring contently. Her cat had not let her out of his sight since she had returned yesterday afternoon. After she set her teacup down, Seymour pushed his head into her hand and meowed. "I missed you too, fur ball. More than you know." Lana ran her fingers through his velvety black fur as he stretched out.

"Sara and Frieda told me all about the trip and how you kept it upbeat, even after everything that happened. Everyone left five-star reviews, even Jess. I do appreciate it."

"Really? I didn't expect Jess to have bothered. That's wonderful news."

"So next week I have a bird-watching tour heading to Costa Rica for ten days. Three more tourists want to join, but I would need another guide to commit before I can book them. What do you say? It is warm and sunny down there this time of year."

"Are you kidding me? Two of your guests died on my first tour."

"You didn't kill them. That was just bad luck."

"But I have to..." What did she have to do exactly? Seymour was in excellent hands with Dotty. Willow could easily fill her one-hour-a-week teaching slot. And Lana already had enough gift cards to feed her chai habit for several months.

Lana had always dreamed about visiting Central America – the volcanoes, snorkeling, and rainforests sounded magical. What did she have to lose by saying yes? Absolutely nothing.

Sensing her hesitation, Dotty added, "Carl was booked to work a two-week tour around Berlin later in January and an eight-day trip to Paris in February. I sure could use your help with those, as well."

"Dotty, are you certain you trust me?"

"Of course I do! You'll be working with at least one other guide on each trip. The Costa Rica tour is a big group, so there will be three other guides present. All are quite experienced. And one is pretty cute." Dotty winked as she took another sip of tea. "So, what do you say?"

"Yes. I would absolutely love to work on all three tours." Lana's eyes widened in excitement. Her passport was going to get quite a workout! She had been dreading returning to Seattle and having to look for work. The only consolation had been that she didn't have to worry about paying rent for three months. So far, this new year was a vast improvement over the past one.

"Excellent. I must say, one of the men taking the Costa Rica trip is quite hunky."

"Is hunky even a word, Dotty?"

"Oh, I don't know. But it should be. So, let me tell you about him. He seems quite athletic. I bet he works out a lot. And he requested that we include a kayaking trip along the coast, as part of the tour."

"A kayaker? That does sound good," Lana leaned back into Dotty's overstuffed couch, one hand holding a cup of tea while the other stroked Seymour's soft fur. As she listened to her friend outline why this guest might just be Lana's perfect match, a smile played on her lips.

Life was so much better with good friends.

THE END

Thank you for reading my novel!
Reviews really do help readers decide whether they want to take a chance on
a new author. If you enjoyed this story, please consider posting a review on
BookBub, Goodreads, Facebook, or with your favorite retailer.
I appreciate it! Jennifer S. Alderson

About the Author

Jennifer S. Alderson was born in San Francisco, raised in Seattle, and currently lives in Amsterdam. After traveling extensively around Asia, Oceania, and Central America, she moved to Darwin, Australia, before finally settling in the Netherlands. Her background in journalism, multimedia development, and art history enriches her novels. When not writing, she can be found in a museum, biking around Amsterdam, or enjoying a coffee along the canal while planning her next research trip.

Jennifer's love of travel, art, and culture inspires her award-winning Zelda Richardson Mystery series, her Travel Can Be Murder Cozy Mysteries, and her standalone stories.

Book One of the Zelda Richardson Mystery series—*The Lover's Portrait*—is a suspenseful whodunit about Nazi-looted artwork that transports readers to WWII and present-day Amsterdam. Art, religion, and anthropology collide in *Rituals of the Dead* (Book Two), a thrilling artifact mystery set in Papua and the Netherlands. Her pulse-pounding adventure set in the Netherlands, Croatia, Italy, and Turkey—*Marked for Revenge* (Book Three)—is a story about stolen art, the mafia, and a father's vengeance. Book Four—*The Vermeer Deception*—is a WWII art mystery set in Germany and the Netherlands.

The Travel Can Be Murder Cozy Mysteries follow the adventures of tour guide and amateur sleuth Lana Hansen. Book One—*Death on the Danube*—takes Lana to Budapest for a New Year's trip. In *Death by Baguette* (Book Two), Lana escorts five couples on an unforgettable Valentine-themed vacation to Paris. In Book Three—*Death by Windmill*—Lana's estranged mother joins her Mother's Day tour to the Netherlands. In Book Four—*Death by Bagpipes*—Lana accompanies a famous magician and his family to Edinburgh during the Fringe Festival. In Book Five—*Death by Fountain*—Lana has to sleuth out who really killed Randy Wright's ex-girlfriend, before his visit to Rome becomes permanent. In Book Six, *Death by Leprechaun*, needs the luck of the Irish to clear her friend of a crime. In Book Seven—*Death by Flamenco*— Lana has to sleuth out a murderer if she is to dance her way out of a jail sentence. Book Eight, *Death by Gondola*, will be released in April 2022.

Jennifer is also the author of two thrilling adventure novels: *Down and Out in Kathmandu* and *Holiday Gone Wrong*. Her travelogue, *Notes of a Naive Traveler*, is a must-read for those interested in traveling to Nepal and Thailand. All three are available in the *Adventures in Backpacking* box set.

For more information about the author and her upcoming novels, please visit Jennifer's website [www.jennifersalderson.com] or sign up for her newsletter [http://eepurl.com/cWmc29].

Acknowledgments

I am deeply indebted to my husband for his support and encouragement while I wrote, researched, and edited this novel. My son deserves a big kiss for putting up with me writing another book.

My editor, Sadye Scott-Hainchek, also deserves a huge round of applause for helping to make this novel shine. The cover designer for this series, Elizabeth Mackey, constantly amazes me with her gorgeous and fun designs.

My mother and I were lucky enough to spend a week in Budapest together. Our wonderful visit inspired me to use this vibrant city as the backdrop for my first cozy mystery.

Death by Baguette: A Valentine's Day Murder in Paris

Follow the further adventures of Lana Hansen in *Death By Baguette: A Valentine's Day Murder in Paris* – Book Two of the Travel Can Be Murder Mystery Series!

Paris—the city of love, lights … and murder? Join tour guide Lana Hansen as she escorts five couples on an unforgettable Valentine-themed vacation to France! Unfortunately it will be the last trip for one passenger…

Lana Hansen's future is looking bright. She has money in her bank account, a babysitter for her cat, and even a boyfriend. Regrettably she won't get to celebrate Valentine's Day with her new beau, Chad. Instead, she will be leading a "lovers only" tour in France. Luckily for Lana, her best friend, Willow, and her partner will be joining her.

Things go downhill when Lana's new boyfriend shows up in Paris for her tour—with his wife. Chad is not the website developer he claimed to be, but a famous restaurant critic whose love of women rivals his passion for food.

After Chad drops dead during a picnic under the Eiffel Tower, a persistent French detective becomes convinced that he was poisoned. And the inspector's sights are set on several members of the tour—including Lana!

While escorting her group through the cobblestone streets of Montmartre, the grand gardens of Versailles, and the historic Marché des Enfants Rouges market, Lana must figure out who really killed Chad before she has to say *bonjour* to prison and *adieu* to her freedom.

Find direct links to buy *Death by Baguette* on Jennifer's website:

jennifersalderson.com.

Death by Baguette
Chapter One—The Big One

February 1—Seattle, Washington

Lana Hansen awoke in a panic, certain Seattle's long-anticipated, catastrophic earthquake was finally happening. Seymour jumped up on her chest, meowing in fright, as the sharp, tearing sound rippling through her ceiling increased in intensity.

Lana grabbed ahold of her cat and raced outside, scared for her upstairs neighbor's safety, as well as their own. Their two-story farmhouse was one of the oldest wooden homes left in this neighborhood, and Lana was certain it would not survive the "Big One" seismologists had been warning locals about for decades.

Once outside, she surveyed her rented home, surprised to see that the siding was intact. In fact, nothing seemed to be shaking or moving, not even the weeping willow in their front yard. And the piercing noise was gone, too.

Filled with adrenaline and uncertainty, Lana rang Dotty Thompson's doorbell, wanting to make sure her upstairs neighbor had survived the initial shock.

Moments later, Dotty opened the door, her face covered in a thick sheen of sweat. "Lana, why are you in your pajamas? Where are your shoes? You better get in here before you catch a cold," she huffed, clearly out of breath. She was dressed in a leopard-skin spandex top and bright pink tights. A pink headband and leopard-skin legwarmers completed the ensemble.

Around Dotty's legs danced her dogs, Chipper and Rodney—or her "boys" as she preferred to call them. They were dressed in matching pink headbands with tiny leopard-print armbands around their front paws.

"I think we just had an earthquake!" Lana said, frozen in place. "You'd better come outside, in case there are aftershocks."

161

"An earthquake? Are you sure? I didn't feel anything moving, but then I was doing jumping jacks just now," Dotty said as she began springing up and down, the old wooden floorboards groaning and creaking under her weight.

Lana leaned against the doorway. "Were you doing them in your living room?"

"Yes, why?"

Dotty's living room was directly above Lana's bedroom. *So that was the thundering noise*, she realized. Her rush of adrenaline subsided as quickly as it arrived. Lana shivered a little and stepped inside Dotty's hallway. "Never mind about the earthquake. It must have been a crazy dream."

When she followed Dotty into her living room, Lana could immediately feel sweat forming on her brow. "Why is it so hot in here?"

"I turned the heater way up. The warmth is supposed to help burn more calories while doing yoga."

"Why are you exercising so early, anyway? It's not even six," Lana asked as she dropped onto Dotty's couch, Seymour still in her arms. At least, until Rodney and Chipper bolted onto the couch, scaring her cat off.

"Chipper! Rodney! Where are your manners?" Dotty admonished her pets, then waddled off to find Seymour.

The pug and Jack Russell terrier growled at each other as they both tried to climb onto Lana's legs. "Okay, boys, I have enough hands and lap for both of you." Lana petted their backs until they settled into a truce with both of their heads on her lap and a body on each side of her legs.

Dotty soon returned with Lana's cat in her arms and sat down next to her. Seymour flicked his tail against Lana's arm but remained in Dotty's lap.

"I must have overdone it salsa dancing last night because my back sure is complaining. Willow's coming over for an emergency yoga session to help me work out the kinks."

"That's nice of her. So did Willow tell Jane yet, or is she still planning on surprising her?" Lana asked, hoping it was the former rather than the latter.

Dotty had arranged for them to join Lana's next tour—a lovers-only trip to Paris in mid-February. As sweet as it was that Willow wanted to surprise Jane with a week-long vacation to one of the most romantic cities in the world, Lana knew Jane would not appreciate the surprise element. In fact, she suspected that a surprise trip would push Jane over the edge, rather than rekindling their romance.

Jane was a wonderful doctor who had just opened up her own practice and regarded her patients as family, staying on call at all hours for them. Yet she was so dedicated to them, Lana wondered whether Jane would ever make time to start her own, despite saying she wanted to do so.

Willow, on the other hand, had made it clear after her thirty-fifth birthday party last month that she was ready to start in-vitro fertilization this year—but only if Jane agreed to work less. The ultimatum made Jane feel as if she had to choose between her career and children. Both women were stubborn and had dug in their heels, and Lana feared that no resolution was in sight.

Dotty sighed and shook her head. "Willow seems convinced that this trip would be best as a surprise. She thinks Jane wouldn't agree to go, otherwise. She's trying to get one of her doctor friends to cover for her, so Jane won't be able to say no."

"Oh yes she will. Jane may be small and quiet, but she is no pushover. You sure don't want to get on her bad side," Lana said.

"I agree with you there. Last week, I saw her chew out a parking valet for slamming her door too hard. I mean, the windows did shake a bit, but nothing broke or cracked. I swear, he was twice her size but was on the verge of tears by the time she got done with him," Dotty said. "I know you aren't convinced, Lana, but I do think this trip will help their relationship. If they are serious about having a child together, they need to make time to talk things out. A week in Paris might just do the trick. Heck, a week in Timbuktu would probably work, too, as long as they really listen to each other."

Lana started to respond when the doorbell rang.

Dotty set Seymour on the couch next to her and rose. "Speak of the devil. Since you're here, why don't you stay and join in?"

"Sure, why not?" Lana stretched her arms out over her lap, jostling the dogs. They grumbled in irritation, but both stayed put. With her hectic tour schedule, she hadn't done yoga or any other regular exercise for months. The walking tours kept her fit, as did running around helping her guests, but she missed the feeling of burning muscles and sweat on her forehead.

Lana gave Rodney and Chipper a hard scratch on the back then slowly rose. Both the pug and Jack Russell terrier rolled off her lap and curled into balls next to Seymour.

When Dotty led Willow back into the room, Lana stood still, unsure as how to greet her friend.

Willow set her rolled-up yoga mat down and put her hands on her hips. "Howdy, stranger! It's good to see you." She stood on her toes to wrap her arms around Lana's neck.

Lana hugged her back, careful not to pull on Willow's long braids. A wave of shame rolled over her. It wasn't that she had been consciously avoiding Willow since returning from Berlin three weeks earlier, but it was a fact that she had not dropped by her friend's apartment or work as often as she usually did. Willow and Jane were fighting more frequently it was hard for Lana to be around them without taking sides. And the last thing she wanted to do was get involved in their baby discussion.

Truth be told, it wasn't just their squabbling that kept her away. She had recently re-entered the dating scene and met a man with potential, which made her even more sensitive to Willow and Jane's troubles. It was hard to be around a couple fighting when she was in the euphoric phase of a new relationship.

"Willow, it's great to see you, too. I'm so sorry I didn't stay until the end of Jane's birthday party. Were you at the restaurant much longer?" Lana had immediately said yes when Chad, her new beau, asked her out to dinner, only to later realize that Jane's birthday was the same night. In an attempt to combine both, Lana had asked Chad if he would instead meet her at a nearby bar for a nightcap afterwards. However, Lana had forgotten how large Jane's family was; dinners with them took significantly longer than normal, and so she'd had to cut out of Jane's party before the other guests were finished.

Willow pursed her lips and looked away. "No. Her mother started in about kids and how we should hurry up and adopt. Apparently Jane hadn't told her we were going to try IVF first."

Ouch, Lana thought. Jane told her mother everything; excluding this big news was not a good sign. "Well, I'm sure she had a reason for waiting to tell…"

"Okay, girls, enough chitchat." Dotty clapped her hands together as she started to jog in place. "I'm all warmed up, and my back is killing me. What do we do first, Willow?"

Willow unfurled her mat across from Dotty. "We salute the sun."

"Oh, I know this one," Dotty exclaimed, standing in the starting position with her feet together and her palms touching in front of her chest.

Lana stood between her friends and copied their stance.

"Now, ladies, let's do this!"

* * *

Are you enjoying the book so far? Buy *Death by Baguette* now and keep reading! Available as paperback and eBook at your favorite retailers.

Made in the USA
Las Vegas, NV
17 May 2022

49014963R00096